FAREWELL, GUL'SARY!

On a bleak Russian night an old man watches his old horse dying. As the horse weakens the old man recalls the events of their two lives which have been inextricably bound together. Within the unity of the long night, time is telescoped from the years following the end of the war until the present moment. Gul'sary was a magnificent horse, a famous pacer, and his master Tanabai was an idealistic communist. Horse and man had an uncanny understanding. Together they knew love, Gul'sary for the playful filly with the white star on her forehead, and Tanabai for a lovely and sympathetic woman. Both fell on hard times; Gul'sary was broken by new masters and Tanabai was beaten by a cruel winter when the same new masters—bureaucrats in charge of the collective farm—displayed their heartless neglect. At the end of his life, friends dying around him, Tanabai is expelled from the Communist Party. With this night and the death of Gul'sary his isolation is complete.

FAREWELL, GUL'SARY!

(Proshchai, Gul'sary!)

by

CHINGIZ AITMATOV

Translated by
JOHN FRENCH

HODDER AND STOUGHTON

First printed in Great Britain 1970

ISBN 0 340 12864 X

Printed in Great Britain for Hodder and Stoughton Limited, St. Paul's House, Warwick Lane, London, E.C.4, by Cox and Wyman Ltd., London, Reading and Fakenham.

FOR

LYALYA

INTRODUCTION

This is the story of a man, Tanabai, and his horse, Gul'sary, and it comes from the Kirgiz Republic in Soviet Central Asia. Some of the highest mountains in the U.S.S.R. form the border with China on the south-east side of the Republic. There is a wide range of climate from the cold of the eternal snows to the temperate and the seasonal extremes of steppe and near-by desert in the north-west. Sheep- and horse-rearing flourish, silk is produced and crops vary from cotton, grapes and tobacco to sugar-beet and potatoes. The population of the Republic is about two and a half million, of whom nearly a million are of the Kirgiz race.

Since the war there has been much development of industry and exploitation of the mineral resources of Kirgizia, but the story of *Farewell, Gul'sary!* is concerned with the present-day descendants of the nomad farmers, who themselves came from the wandering tribes, headed by feudal lords. The scene of the story is set in the western part of the country, close to the border with the great Kazakh Republic of the U.S.S.R.

Particularly in sheep farming, a form of nomadic husbandry is still practised on the collective farms, although the old *yurtas* have been largely replaced by modern tents and buildings. All the same much of the ancient lore and many old customs remain. The story covers the years from the end of the war until about 1966.

The author, Chingiz Aitmatov, is himself a Kirgiz. He was born in the *kishlak* (settlement) of Sheker in the Kirovskoye *raion* on 12th December, 1928. The root of his family name—Aitmat—means tailor. His grandfather, who was a famous craftsman in metal and leather, especially in the making of saddles, had brought the first sewing machine to Sheker. But in spite of this skill and his fame as a player of the national instrument—the *komuz*, he remained poor. However, his son had

7

the opportunity of learning Russian and later studied in Moscow.

Thus Chingiz Aitmatov's parents, and especially his mother, taught him Russian and introduced him at an early age to Russian literature. At the same time, the young Chingiz's grandmother on his father's side taught him Kirgiz and the wealth of legend, songs and lore of his Kirgiz people. On her death, his aunt continued this part of his education. Then he went to schools, both Russian and Kirgiz. Because of the war, in 1942 he had to leave school early in order to help his mother bring up her four children. He worked in various posts in Sheker on the village's collective farm. Then he went to the veterinary school at Dzhambul, across the border in Kazakhstan, from which he graduated with honours. Later he passed out from the Kirgiz Agricultural Institute as a livestock specialist or *zootekhnik* in 1953. While at the Institute he began his literary career by translating one of the Soviet author Kataev's books into Kirgiz. In 1952 he published his first story—about a Japanese newsboy—*Gazetchik Dzhyuido* ("Newsboy Dzhyuido"). This was followed by *Ashym* in 1953, but in 1956 he gave up his farm work and entered the Higher course of Literature of the Union of Writers in Moscow. In 1957 *Litsom k litsu* ("Face to face") appeared and in 1958, just before he left the Institute, he published *Dzhamilya*. This story, about a young woman of that name, has been translated into at least forty-two languages of Europe, Asia and Africa. The French translation was made by Louis Aragon in 1959 and of it he wrote, "For me this is the most beautiful love story in the world."

After a short period as editor of *Literaturny Kirgiztan*, in 1960 Aitmatov became a correspondent of *Pravda*. In 1962 his stories *Pervy uchitel'* ("First teacher") and *Materinskoye pole* ("Mother's field") appeared. The first became the base of a film of that name and the latter bears a dedication to his parents in the following words:

Father, I know not where you are buried.
I dedicate this to you, Torekul Aitmatov;
Mama, you brought up all four of us,
I dedicate this to you, Nagima Aitmatova.

In 1963 Aitmatov received a Lenin Prize for literature for his *Povesti gor i stepei* ("Stories of the mountains and steppes"). In Surkov's *Short Literary Encyclopaedia* Chingiz Aitmatov's writing is described as follows:

"A story true to life, simplicity, grace and poetry make up the qualities of his works."

He has the title of People's Writer of the Kirgiz S.S.R. and is president of the Directorate of the Union of Cinematographers of Kirgizia.

Most of Aitmatov's stories are written in Kirgiz, but *Farewell, Gul'sary!* was originally written in Russian and published in 1966 in a somewhat shorter form in the controversial literary magazine *Novy Mir*. Later Aitmatov became a member of the editorial board. *Farewell, Gul'sary!*, for which he received a State Prize in 1968, has also been published in book form—in 1967 in a collection of his stories published in Frunze, the capital of the Kirgiz S.S.R., and on its own in Moscow in 1968. It has been translated into Bulgarian and German.

A new story by Chingiz Aitmatov has been published in *Novy Mir* in 1970.

F. J. F.

GLOSSARY

ail a village or settlement.

Akbai, Kokbai a child's jingle.

aksakal a village elder; used as a respectful greeting by a man to an older man.

alaman see *baiga*.

-apa mother; when preceded by the woman's name used as a form of address by children, e.g. Dzhaidar-apa.

Aleikum-assalom the answer to the greeting "*Assalom-aleikum*".

arbaki spirits of the ancestors.

Assalom-aleikum "Peace be unto you!"

bai a landlord; now used rather as "sir" between equals.

baibiche wife of a *bai;* preceded by her name, used in addressing a man's wife.

baiga a contest on horseback; *alaman-baiga,* a free-for-all contest involving a goat-skin as the object of contention.

barin a lord, master; used also sarcastically in the sense a "grand gentleman".

batiry raiding marauders.

Chapaev a hero of the Civil War.

dombra a Kazakh musical instrument.

duldul a wonderful horse of legend.

dzhigit a young horseman, hence a bold young man.

Gaz abbreviation for the *G*orky *A*utomobile Factory (*Z*avod), a make of truck.

kamcha a whip.

karagach a species of tree, elm type.

-ke (-ake) used as a suffix to the first syllables of a man's name

as a friendly or affectionate form of address, e.g. Tanabai
becomes Tanake.

khurda   a wasting disease of animals.

kishen   old-fashioned metal fetters.

kolkhoz   shortened form of words for collective farm, headed by
a *predsedatel'* (chairman or president).

komsomol   shortened form of words for Young Communist
League; a member of that organisation, or used adjectivally.

komuz   a three-stringed instrument, see also *temir-komuz*.

kul   a slave.

kulak   a rich peasant, a class liquidated in the twenties.

kumys   fermented mare's milk.

lapsha   a noodle-like dish.

manap   a feudal lord in a nomad tribe; used later to denote
an exploiter. The term used by Tanabai of Segizbaev.

mazhara   a large cart, often drawn by oxen.

Oibaiai, baurymai   a mourning cry.

obkom   abbreviation for *oblast'* (q.v.) committee of the Communist Party.

oblast'   an administrative region, based on a large town, an area
larger than a *raion* (q.v.).

partorg   the Party affairs organiser at a farm or any other small
institution or group.

rab   a slave.

raion   region; an administrative area based on a medium-sized
town.

raikom   abbreviation for regional (the *raion*) committee of the
Communist Party.

sakmanshchitsa (pl. -*y*)   a woman helper sent to the sheep farms
during the lambing season.

sovkhoz   shortened form of the words for State farm.

temir-komuz   a Kirgiz pizzicato musical instrument in the form
of an iron ring with a steel vibrating tongue in the centre.

ukruk   a stick with a noose on it, used in horse catching.

valenki   felt boots.

yefreitor   lance-corporal.

yurta   a nomad tent made from a wooden frame covered with a felt sheeting.

versta   (pl. -*y*) a measurement of distance, about 1,200 yards.

zavkhoz   abbreviation for the manager of a farm activity, e.g. the horse breeding, within a collective or State farm.

N.B. Throughout the text comrade and party are spelt without capitals following common Soviet usage.

FAREWELL, GUL'SARY !

I

The old man was riding on an old cart. And Gul'sary, the pacer who drew it was an old, a very old horse.

The road climbed endlessly up to the plateau. Among the grey desert hillocks the winter wind swirled continually but in summer it was as hot as hell.

For Tanabai this climb was always torture. He hated travelling slowly—he just could not stand it. In his younger days he had to make the journey to the regional town fairly often and on the way back he would force the horse to gallop up the hill. He lashed it without pity. When he travelled with the others on the *mazhara*, especially if it was being pulled by oxen, he would jump off as it went along. Seizing his bundle of clothes, he would hurry ahead on foot without a word. He walked at a furious pace, as if he was leading an attack, stopping only when he reached the plateau where he would wait, breathing deeply, as the cart crawled up the long slope. In spite of a sharp pain in his heart and a stitch from the fast walk, it was far better than being dragged up on the ox-cart.

When he was alive his friend Choro used to chaff him for his eccentricity. He would say, "Do you want to know, Tanabai, why you never get anywhere? You're too impatient for God's sake, you always have to go faster and faster. You want world revolution at once! Not only the normal pace of revolution, but even the ordinary road, the slope out of Aleksandrovka is too much for you. Everyone else just rides quietly along, but you must jump out . . . and race up the hill as if wolves were at your heels. And where does it get you? Nowhere! You still have to sit and wait up there for the rest of us. And you won't achieve world revolution on your own like that—you'll have to wait for everyone else."

But that was long, long ago.

On this occasion Tanabai did not even notice that he had

climbed the hill out of Aleksandrovka. It seemed he was getting used to old age so he just kept jogging on. Nowadays he always made the journey on his own. It was no use searching out the gang he used to travel with over this noisy road. One had been killed in the war, another had just died, another was sitting at home living out his days. The young ones all went by lorry. None of them wanted to drag along with him and his old horse.

The wheels clattered over the old road. They would go on clattering for a long time yet. Ahead lay the steppe, and there beyond the canal began the long climb into the foothills.

He had noticed a long time ago that his old pacer, Gul'sary or Buttercup, because of his light yellow coat, was beginning to falter and weaken. But immersed in his own gloomy thoughts, he was not unduly worried.

Surely the horse could not collapse on the way? He would get them both home, somehow . . .

Indeed how could he know that Gul'sary had made the climb up from Aleksandrovka for the last time in his life and was now covering his final *versty*? The horse's head was swimming, as if he was doped; in his fading vision the earth was turning around him in a strange bright light and tilting from side to side. For the old horse, Gul'sary, the road ahead from time to time seemed to end in a dark nothingness, and there before him, where the mountains should be, a reddish mist, or perhaps smoke, seemed to be rising and falling.

For a long time the horse had felt a dull ache in his straining heart and it was harder and harder for him to breathe in his heavy collar. The breech band was cutting into him, and on the left side under the collar something sharp was hurting him. Perhaps it was a thorn or the end of a nail protruding through the felt of the collar. The open sore on his shoulder was burning, it itched unbearably. His legs were becoming heavier and heavier as if he was moving over wet, soggy ploughland.

But the old horse went on and on, wearing himself out, and the old man, Tanabai, occasionally urged him on, and jerking the reins, was thinking his own thoughts. He had, indeed, much to think about.

The wheels rattled on the old road. Gul'sary still went on at his usual pace, that same rhythm, that special trot, which he had never lost since the first time he had got up on his feet and unsteadily trotted off after his mother—a big heavily-maned mare.

Gul'sary was a pacer from birth and his famous gait had brought him both good days and bad during his life. Earlier no one would have dreamed of harnessing him to a cart; that would have been sacrilege. But, as the saying goes, in a crisis a young man will wade a ford still in his boots, just as a horse will drink with his bridle on.

All this was in the past and far behind. Now the pacer was coming to the end of his journey with his last remaining strength. He had never moved so slowly at the end of his journey, yet never had he approached it so quickly. The end was only a step away from him all the time.

The wheels rattled on the old road.

The feeling that the ground beneath his hooves was insecure brought back to the horse's fading memory those far-off summer days, that wet, uneven meadow in the mountains, that wonderful and unbelievable world in which the sun seemed to neigh at him and race over the mountains. As a silly young foal he had raced after the sun across the meadow, across the stream, through the bushes until the stallion of his herd, with his angry lowered ears, had caught up with him and turned him back. In those far-off days it had seemed that the herds were walking upside-down in a deep lake, and his mother—the big mare with the heavy mane—seemed to turn into a warm, milky cloud. He loved that moment when his mother suddenly turned into a gentle, quietly snorting cloud. Her teats became firm and sweet, the milk foamed on his lips and he choked with its abundance and sweetness. He loved to stand there nuzzling at her. What ravishing, heady milk it was! His whole world—the sun, earth and his mother—was contained in a gulp of that milk. And even when he was sated, he could still enjoy one more gulp, and another, and another.

Alas, this time did not last. Soon everything changed. The sun stopped neighing in the sky and jumping over the mountains; it rose sedately in the east and went unerringly round to the west; the herds ceased to walk around upside-down and the meadow, trampled under their hooves, became dark and the stones in the shallows clattered and broke. The big mare turned out to be a stern mother and bit him painfully on the withers when he worried her too much. There was not enough milk and he had to begin to eat grass. That life was beginning which was to span the long years and which was now drawing to its close.

In all his long life the pacer had never returned to that summer. It was lost for ever. He had been saddled, travelled many roads and tracks with many different riders and there had been no end to the journeys which he had made. Only now, when the sun again moved from its place and the earth was unsteady under his feet, when he was dazzled and unable to see clearly, that summer which he had lost so long ago seemed to have returned to him. There were the mountains; that wet meadow, the herds of horses, that great mare with her mane. They were all before his eyes in a rippling, shimmery light.

And with a great effort, stretching hard, he desperately moved his legs in an effort to drag himself from the harness collar and the shafts, to re-enter that world of the past so suddenly once more before him. But each time the vision faded and this was torture. His mother called him (with a quiet neigh) as she had when he was a foal; the other horses raced past brushing him with their flanks and tails and yet he had not enough strength to conquer the glittering haze of the snow flurry which played around him all the more. It whipped around him, filling his eyes and nostrils with snow; he was sweating and shivering all at the same time with cold as the unattainable world of his past quietly buried itself and vanished among the eddies of snow. The mountains, the meadow, the river and the other horses had vanished. Only dimly ahead could he see the great shadow of his mother. She did not want to leave him. She called him and he neighed back with all his might, sobbing, but not a sound came and she could not hear his voice. Then everything, even the snow disappeared.

The wheels stopped clattering.

The wound under his collar stopped aching. The pacer halted, staggering from side to side. His eyes were hurting and a strange sound was drumming in his head.

Tanabai threw down the reins and climbed down unsteadily; he stretched his cramped legs and went gloomily up to the horse.

20

"Eh, what the devil's up with you?" he swore quietly as he looked at the horse.

The horse stood with his huge head and thin scrawny neck drooping from the collar. The ribs rose and fell, stiffly moving the thin flabby flanks. Once light lemon, even gold, the horse was now brown from sweat and dirt. The grey streams of sweat dripped in lathering profusion from the bony croup on to the belly, down the legs and on to the hooves.

"It isn't as if I had driven you hard," mumbled Tanabai as he began to fuss. He eased off the girth, undid the hame strap and unharnessed the horse. The bit was covered in thick foam. He wiped the horse's head and neck with his sleeve. Then he went quickly to the cart, gathered up about half an armful of hay, and put it at the horse's feet. But the horse made no move towards it, he just shivered.

Tanabai picked up a handful.

"Go on, take it, eat it, come on."

The horse's lips moved but could not grasp the hay. Tanabai looked into the eyes and frowned. He could see nothing in the deep-set eyes, half covered by the bare lids. The eyes were dark and empty like the windows of an empty house.

Tanabai looked round in despair; in the distance were the mountains; all around was the bare steppe and not a soul in sight along the road. At this time of year there were few enough travellers about.

The old horse and the old man stood alone on the empty deserted road.

It was the end of February. The snow had already disappeared from the plain; only in the secret haunts of winter, in the ravines and the reedy gullies lingered the spines of the last snowdrifts, looking like a wolf's backbone. The wind bore a faint smell of old snow and the earth was still frozen, grey and moribund. The miserable, inhospitable stony steppe stood at the end of the winter. Just at the sight of it Tanabai felt frozen inside.

Shaking his dishevelled grey beard and shading his eyes with the matted sleeve of his coat, he gazed for a long time towards the west. The sun, partially covered by clouds, was resting on the horizon. Already the dim misty sunset was beginning. There was no sign of especially threatening weather, but all the same it was

cold and unpleasant. "If I had known, I would not have left,"
grieved Tanabai. "Now I'm stuck here in the open, unable
to go one way or the other. I will have done the horse to death
unnecessarily."

Yes, he should have started back tomorrow morning. Then if
anything had happened on the way by day, someone could have
helped him. But he had left after midday; he just should not
have done that at this time of the year.

Tanabai climbed up on to a near-by hillock—was there a car
coming in the distance?—no, there was nothing to be seen and he
wandered back to the cart.

"I was a fool to leave," thought Tanabai, again blaming himself for his perpetual impatience and hurry. He was ashamed and
angry with himself and everything which had forced him to
hurry away from his son's house. Of course, he should have
stayed the night and let the horse rest. But what had he done
. . .?

Tanabai angrily shook his head.

"No, I couldn't have stayed. I would have rather walked," he
defended himself. "Could anyone really talk to a father-in-law as
she did? Whatever else I may be, I am, after all, his father. Why
did I become a party member, if I was to spend all my life looking
after the sheep and horses, and then to be thrown out in my old
age . . .? What kind of a son is he? He kept quiet and didn't dare
look me in the eye. She'll say to him, "Renounce your father,"
and he'll do it! What a wet fish—and he crawls to the authorities,
too! What can one say? What are people coming to today?"

Tanabai had become quite hot; he undid his shirt front and,
breathing heavily, began to walk around the cart, forgetting
about his horse, the road, the journey and the oncoming night.
He just could not calm down. In his son's house he had been able
to control himself for he thought it below his dignity to quarrel
with his daughter-in-law. But now he was in a rage; now he
could have said everything to her that he had thought out so
bitterly on the way.

"You did not admit me to the party and you did not expel me.
How could you know, daughter-in-law, how things were then.
Now anyone can criticise; now everyone is educated and you are
honoured and respected. But they were always making demands

on us, endless demands. We had to answer for our father, mother, friend, enemy, ourselves, the neighbour's dog; we had to answer for everything on earth! It's none of your business that I was expelled. That's my sorrow, daughter! It's no concern of yours. It's none of your business." He went on in this way as he stood by the cart. "It's none of your business," he repeated again. And the worst of it all and the most humiliating thing about it was that there was really nothing else to say except "Mind your own business".

He went on walking round and round the cart until he remembered that something had to be done, he couldn't stay there all night.

Gul'sary stood there, quite still and quite indifferent to everything, stiffly hunched with his legs together; it seemed as if he was already dead.

"What's up?" Tanabai hurried over to him and listened to the horse's laboured groaning.

"You dozed off? You are in a bad way, old man! It is bad, isn't it?"

He felt the cold ears and put his hand under the mane where it was also cold and damp. But what frightened him most of all was that he could not feel the usual weight of the mane.

"You've really got old; your mane is as light as a feather. We're all growing old, all going the same way home," he thought bitterly. And he got up undecidedly, not knowing what to do. If he left the horse by the cart and went on by foot, he could be at home in the ravine by midnight. He lived there with his wife; the water board watcher lived about a mile away down river. In the summer Tanabai superintended the haymaking. In the winter he kept an eye on the ricks to see that the shepherds did not cart off the hay too early or spoil it in any way.

Last autumn he had gone up to the office one day when the new brigadier, a young economist, looked in and said to him:

"Go, *aksakal*, to the stable; we have got a new horse for you. True enough he's old, but he'll do for your work."

"What sort is it?" asked Tanabai cautiously, "another old crock?"

"They will show you. He's a sort of light dun, you should know him well; once upon a time you used to ride him."

23

Tanabai went over to the stable and the sight of the pacer in the yard wrung his heart. "We've met up again at last, it seems," he said to the worn-out, old horse. He did not have it in his heart to refuse to take the horse and so he led him away home.

There his wife hardly recognised the horse.

"Tanabai, is it really our Gul'sary?" She was astonished.

"It's the very same . . ." mumbled Tanabai trying to avoid looking into his wife's eyes. They could not afford to indulge in reminiscences about the pacer; Tanabai had had much to answer for in his past. To avoid an unpleasant discussion, he spoke roughly to her.

"What are you standing there for? Go and heat us up some food. I'm as hungry as a dog."

"Yes, I'm looking," she answered, "and thinking just what old age means. If you hadn't told me it was the same old Gul'sary, I wouldn't have recognised him."

"What's there to be surprised about? Do you think that either of us look any better? Everyone grows older."

"That's just what I was thinking." She shook her head and laughing good-naturedly said, 'Perhaps you will want to go riding around again at night. I'll let you."

"What's the use?"

He waved her away and turned his back to her. He could give her a joke for a joke, but in embarrassment he went into the shed to get some hay and spent a long time in there. He had thought that she had forgotten all about that, but she had not.

Smoke was pouring from the chimney and his wife was heating up the dinner which had got cold. He was fussing around with the hay when she called him.

"Come on in, or the meal will get cold again."

She had no more to say about the past. What, indeed, was there to be said?

All that autumn and winter Tanabai had tended the horse, feeding him with hot bran mash and sliced sugar-beet. Gul'sary's teeth were worn right down and only the stumps remained. Now when he had just got the horse back into condition, this had happened. No, he had not the heart to leave the horse by the roadside.

24

"Well, Gul'sary, shall we try and get going?"

Tanabai gave him a push, the horse staggered and moved his feet apart. "Wait a moment." With the whip Tanabai lifted up the sack in which he had taken some potatoes to his daughter-in-law and got his basket out from under it. His wife had baked him some things for the journey but he had forgotten all about them—he had just not felt like eating. Tanabai broke off half a small cake and crushed it into his old jacket and offered the crumbs to the horse. Gul'sary noisily sniffed in the aroma of the flour but could not eat. Then Tanabai fed him with his hand. He put several pieces into the horse's mouth and Gul'sary began to chew them.

"Eat up, eat it up and perhaps we'll get home, eh?"

Tanabai felt happier.

"If we go quietly, take it slowly and easily, perhaps we'll get home. Everything will be all right there and with the help of my old woman we'll get you well again," he said persuasively. Saliva from the horse's lips dripped on to his hands and Tanabai was glad that it was warm. Then he took the horse by the bridle.

"Off we go, no need to stand still. We're off," he ordered decisively.

The pacer moved off, the cart squeaked and the wheels clattered slowly on the road. And they walked slowly, old man and old horse.

"He's so weak," thought Tanabai about the horse as he walked alongside him.

"How old are you, Gul'sary? Twenty? Perhaps more; yes. I'm sure you're more than twenty."

25

2

The first time that they had met was after the war. *Yefreitor*
Tanabai Bakasov had served both on the western and the eastern
fronts and was demobilised after the capitulation of the Kwan-
tung Army. Altogether he was in the forces about six years. All
in all God had been good to him; once he was concussed in
a cart and another time he was wounded by a splinter in the
chest, was two months in hospital before once again rejoining
his unit.

And when he got home the women selling food at the stations
called him "old man". But this was really a joke and Tanabai
was not very upset by it. He was not very young, of course, but
then he was not old either, he just looked older. He had got a
weathered brown complexion during the war and his whiskers
had gone grey, but in body and in spirit he was still strong. A
year later his wife gave him a daughter and then a second. Both
were now married with children. They often visited the parents in
the summer. The husband of the elder was a driver; he would
put everyone into the van and off they went up into the mountains to see the old people. No, he could not ask for more from his
daughters and sons-in-law, but his own son ... that was another
story.

On the journey home after victory it seemed as if a real life
was just beginning. It gladdened his heart. At the big stations
along the line the train was met and sent on its way by orches-
tras. At home his wife was waiting with their son who was then
seven and about to start school; Tanabai felt as if he was reborn,
as if he could discount everything which had gone before. He
wanted to forget about the past and to think only of the future.
It all seemed clear and simple; he had to bring up the children,
get back to a regular job, build a house, in short—he just had to
live. And nothing ought to interfere with this because all the past
had been pledged for the real life ahead for which everyone had

striven and for which they had conquered and many had died in the war.

But it seemed that Tanabai was in a hurry; he was in too much of a hurry and he had still more and more years to give in pledge for the future.

At first he worked in a smithy, wielding a hammer. He had once had some experience of this work, and having got to the anvil, he would strike with all his might from morning until evening, so that the smith scarcely had time to turn over the red-hot metal under his blows. Even now he could hear the rhythm of the hammer blows and the ringing noise of the smithy which used to calm all his worries and cares. Either there was a shortage of bread or clothes, or women were still going about in galoshes or just barefoot, or the children hardly saw sugar. Everyone at the collective farm was in debt and bank accounts were frozen—but he was able to get right away from all these cares with his hammer. He would grunt, the anvil would ring, the blue sparks fly. "Uh-a, uh-a," he breathed, lifting up and bringing down the hammer, continually thinking, "We won, we won," and the hammer blow echoed this thought.

Not only Tanabai but everyone else in those days lived on the feeling of victory as if it were bread.

Later on Tanabai went to work as a herdsman up in the mountains. Choro persuaded him to do this. Choro, now dead, was then the president of the collective farm, the *kolkhoz*, as he had been all through the war. He was not called up because of his weak heart. He just sat at home and aged a lot. Tanabai had noticed this at once when he got back home again.

No one else could have persuaded him to change from his work at the smithy to be a herdsman. But Choro was his oldest friend. Long ago as young communists together, they had persuaded the people to join the collective farms and together they had turned out the *kulaks*. Tanabai had been very active in that work, showing no mercy to those who were on the eviction list.

Choro dropped in at the smithy, succeeded in persuading him and was delighted, "I was afraid that you had grown attached to your hammer and couldn't let it go," he smiled.

Choro was ill and gaunt, his neck was long and his face was

lined. Although it was a warm day in summer, Choro was in his usual sweater.

They sat there, crouching on their haunches by the ditch near the smithy and talked. Tanabai thought to himself what Choro had been like in his youth. Then he had been the best educated person in the village and quite a coming lad. People respected him for his quiet, kindly manner. But Tanabai did not approve his good-nature. At a meeting he would jump up and pick holes in Choro and criticise his insufferable gentleness to the class enemy. His speech might have come straight out of the newspapers. He could repeat by heart all he had heard read out. Sometimes he even frightened himself with what he said. Such was the force of his words.

"You know," said Choro, "I have just spent three days up in the mountains. The old men were asking if the soldiers had all come home. I said yes, all those who were still alive. Then they asked me what was the hold-up in getting them back to work. I told them that they were already at work, some farming, some building and the others all busy somewhere. Then they said, 'We know all about that but who is to look after the herds? Of course they can wait until we die, but that's not far off now.

"I was ashamed. You realise what they were getting at? In the war we had sent these old men up into the mountains as herdsmen. And there they had stayed. I don't need to tell you that it's no work for old men. You're in the saddle the whole time and there is no let-up day or night. And as for the winter nights! Do you remember Derbishbai—he was the one who got frozen stiff in the saddle. Then there is the breaking-in which they had had to do, for the army needed the horses. Try it when you're seventy —let some four-footed devil take you up hill and down dale, you'd never collect your bones together again. They deserve all praise that they've stuck at it so long. Now the troops are back, but with the grand ideas and the culture they've picked up abroad, they turn up their noses at a herdsman's job, they just don't want to do it, 'Why should we roam about the mountains on a horse?' That's how it is. Help us out, Tanabai. You go up there and we'll be able to make others do the same."

"All right, Choro. I will try and persuade my wife to agree," answered Tanabai. But he thought to himself, "Life has stormed around you, Choro, but you are still the same. You burn with kindness. Perhaps that is just as well. We've seen everything during the war, that may make us kinder to one another now. Maybe that is the main thing in life?"

They would have gone their ways and Tanabai was already walking back to the smithy, but Choro suddenly called after him, "Wait a moment, Tanabai." He rode up, leaned from the saddle and looked at his friend and spoke quietly.

"You're not angry are you, Tanabai?" he asked. "You know I have so very little time now. I wanted to sit and have a heart-to-heart as we used to do. We've not seen one another for so long. I thought that when the war was over things would be easier, but instead there are more problems. Even if you shut your eyes there are still things to be thought over—how to improve the work, feed the people and fulfil the plans. And the people are not what they were—they want a better life too . . ."

But they never succeeded in having that heart-to-heart talk, and never got the chance to sit down alone. Time passed and then it was too late . . .

Thus it was that Tanabai went up to the mountains to work as a herdsman, and where he saw for the first time in old Torgoi's herd, the dun colt.

"What are you leaving me, *aksakal*? The herd's nothing special, is it?" Tanabai teased the old herdsman, when they had counted the horses and let them out of the corral.

Torgoi was a dry little old man without a single whisker on his wrinkled face and came just up to one's elbow, like a boy. His great shaggy sheepskin hat on top made him look like a toadstool. Such old men are usually easily roused, quarrelsome and vociferous.

But Torgoi was not going to swallow the bait.

"Well, it is a herd, just like any other," he said coolly. "There's nothing particular to write home about, but as you work with them, you'll see."

"Yes, I will, father," said Tanabai in conciliatory agreement.

"But there is one!" Torgoi raised the brim of his hat from his eyes and standing up in his stirrups, pointed with his whip handle.

29

"Look at that dun colt, grazing over there on the right. He'll go far."

"That one? That round one over there with the silky coat and the short loins?"

"He was a late one. But he'll catch up, he'll be a beauty."

"What's he got? What's so special about him?"

"He has been a pacer from the moment he was foaled."

"Well?"

"You see few of them. In the old days he would have been priceless. People would have fought to the death for one like that."

"Let's have a closer look!" suggested Tanabai.

They spurred their horses, circled the herd and cut off the dun and drove him before them. The colt was not averse to a chance for a run. He cheerfully shook his forelock, neighed and as if he was run by clockwork, started off with his accurate, fast pace and made a great semi-circle in order to get back to the herd. Tanabai was delighted with the way the horse moved and began to shout:

"Oh, look how he moves! Look at him!"

"What did you expect?" said the old herdsman, perkily.

They trotted after the pacer and shouted like children at a fair. Their voices seemed to urge on the colt, he went faster and faster, effortlessly as if he was flying, with not one false step.

They had to break their horses into a gallop, but the colt continued with his pacer's action.

"You see, Tanabai!" shouted Torgoi, waving his hat, "He's sensitive to the voice, quick like a knife in the hand; watch how he reacts to a shout! Oi! Oi! Oi!"

When the dun colt had returned to the herd at last, they left him alone. But for a long time they could not calm down as they let their overheated horses cool.

"Thank you Torgoi, you've raised a fine little horse there. It does one's heart good to see him."

'He's a good one, touch wood," agreed the old man, "but take care." He became serious and scratched the back of his neck. "Ride him yourself in the spring and above all, don't gossip about him. There are as many hunters after a pacer as there are after a pretty young girl. If a girl falls into good hands, she'll flourish and delight the eyes. But if she get's a wrong-un, you can only suffer when you see her. And you cannot do a thing to help. It's the same with a good horse. It is easy to ruin him and he will fall in full gallop."

"Don't worry, *aksakal*, I'm not callow, I understand a bit of this business."

"Well that's good. His name, by the way, is Gul'sary. Got it?"

"Gul'sary?"

"Yes. My little granddaughter stayed with us last summer. That's her name for him. She fell in love with him. He was only a little foal then. But remember: Gul'sary."

Old man Torgoi proved to be talkative. He spent the whole night giving instructions. Tanabai listened patiently.

He accompanied Torgoi and his wife for some seven *versty* from the settlement. There was an empty *yurta* in which he and his family were to live and in the other his assistant would live but they had not yet picked him. So for the present he would be on his own.

As they said good-bye, Torgoi reminded him again.

"Don't touch the dun yet. And don't trust him to anyone else. Yes, and go carefully with him. When you get him saddled don't push him too hard at first. If you nag him, he'll spoil his action and you'll have ruined the horse. And during the early days see that he doesn't drink when he's hot. The water goes to their feet and they can get inflamed. But when you do go out on him, come and show him to me, unless I die first."

And so Torgoi and his old wife went away, leaving him the herd, the *yurta,* the mountains, and taking with them their camel laden with all their possessions . . .

If only Gul'sary had known about all this talk and how much more was still to come and to what end all this would lead . . .

He still wandered free in the herd as before. All around him were the same mountains, grass and streams. Only, instead of the old man, there was another master in a grey overcoat and in a soldier's cap with flaps. The new master's voice was a bit hoarse, but loud and commanding. The herd soon got used to him. Let him fuss around, if it made him happy.

Later on the snow started. It fell often and settled. The horses scratched at the snow with their hooves to reach the grass. The master's face got black and his hands oak-hard from the wind. Now he was going around in *valenki* and wrapped himself up in a big fur coat. Gul'sary had grown his long winter coat but even with that he was cold, especially at night. In the freezing nights the herd gathered together in a dense body and stood until sunrise all covered with frost. The master rode around them, clapped his hands together and rubbed his face. Sometimes he would disappear and then return again. It was far better when he did not go away. Whenever he shouted or groaned from the cold, the herd lifted their heads and pricked their ears, but once they were sure that their master was near them, they dozed off again in the rustling and whistling of the night wind. After that winter Gul'sary was to remember Tanabai's voice for the rest of his life.

One night a storm blew up in the mountains. Stinging snow fell. It gathered in the mane, weighed down the tail and blocked the eyes. The herd was all on edge. Horses pressed together and shivered. The old mares snorted uneasily and pushed the foals to the centre of the herd for safety. But Gul'sary got pushed to the outside and could not get back to the other young ones. Then he was in real trouble and began to kick and push. The stallion leader of the herd had been circling around, cutting up the snow with his hooves and pushing the herd tighter and tighter together into a pack. Sometimes he would race off to one side, shaking his head and flattening down his ears in an aggressive way, disappearing into the darkness so that only his snorts could be heard until, wickedly angry, he came back to the others. When he saw that Gul'sary was off on his own, he charged up to him, striking him with his chest and then, turning away, gave him a powerful kick in the side with his mighty hind legs.

This hurt Gul'sary so much that he nearly suffocated. Deep inside him something seemed to crack, he shrieked from the blow and almost fell. That stopped him from trying to go off on his own. He stood there obediently keeping close to the rest of the herd with an aching pain in his side and aching hate in his heart for the ferocious stallion. The horses were quiet again and then suddenly he heard a dull drawn-out howling. He had never heard the wolves howling before, but all at once everything deep

32

inside him seemed to stop and turn to ice. The herd shivered, alert, and listened. There was complete silence all round. But it was a terrible silence. The snow went on falling, rustling on Gul'sary's raised head. Where was their master? How they longed to have him around now, just to hear his voice and to breathe in the smoky smell of his fur coat. But he was not there. Gul'sary glanced to one side and froze with horror. Over there a shadowy form could be seen creeping over the snow in the darkness. Gul'sary gave a sudden start and the herd dashed off at once in full career. With wild screams and neighing the maddened horses made off like an avalanche into the pitch darkness. There was no power on earth that could stop them. The herd raced away carrying one another along like the stones in a rock fall high up in the mountains.

Bewildered, Gul'sary sped on in the wild rush. Suddenly there was a shot and then another. As they ran the horses heard the angry yell of their master's voice. It seemed to come first from one side, then from the other and cutting across their path, suddenly from dead ahead. They were now overtaking the incessant cry, it was leading them. Their master was with them. He rode ahead, risking at any moment a fall from a precipice or into a ravine. Now he lessened his cry, then he became quite hoarse, still shouting on "Kait, kait, kaita-a-ait!" And they galloped on after him to save themselves from the terror behind.

Towards dawn Tanabai had driven the herd back to their old place. Only there did the horses stop. There was a thick steamy mist over the herd as the horses panted and still shivered from fright. They bit at the snow with their hot lips. Tanabai also was eating the snow. He sat on his haunches and crammed the cold white lumps into his mouth by the handful. Then he suddenly seemed to go rigid and fell forward with his head on his arms. And the snow still fell from the sky, melting on the hot backs of the horses and dripping down in muddy, yellow drops . . .

The deep snow melted, the earth appeared again, became green and Gul'sary grew in strength. The horses lost their winter coats and new hair appeared. It was as if the winter and the hunger had never been. The horses did not remember all this, but the man did. He remembered the night of the wolves when he was stiff with cold as he rode in the saddle and bit his lips so as not to cry out as he sat by the fire thawing his frozen hands and feet; he remembered the spring which brought the clear ice covering the earth with a leaden crust. He remembered how the weaklings in the herd had died and, after coming down from the mountains, he had with downcast eyes signed in the office the reports about the loss of the horses and all at once he had exploded with rage, shouted and struck the desk of the president with his fist:

"Don't look at me like that! I'm not some fascist! Where are the stables for the herds, where is the feed, the corn and the salt? We have nothing but the wind to hold on to! Were we meant to run our work like that? Look at the torn clothes we have to wear! Look at our *yurtas*, look at the conditions under which I live! We don't even get enough bread. At the front we were a hundred times better off. And you go on looking at me as if I had strangled these horses!"

He remembered the strange silence of the president, his greying face. He remembered how he was ashamed of his words and he began to apologise.

"Forgive, forgive me, I lost my temper," he stuttered and forced the words out.

"It is you who should forgive me," said Choro.

And he became even more ashamed when the president called in the storekeeper and ordered:

"Give him five kilos of flour."

"What about the crêches?"

"What crêches? You are always getting things wrong, give it to him!" Choro commanded tersely.

Tanabai wanted to refuse point-blank. Soon indeed the milk would start and there would be *kumys*; but looking at the president and guessing how he had been deceived, he nevertheless said nothing. Then every time afterwards he burnt his tongue on the *lapsha* from that flour. He would throw down the spoon.

"What are you up to? Do you want to scald me?"

"Let it get cooler, you're not a baby," said his wife calmly.

He remembered, he remembered it all ...

But it was now already May. The stallions were calling, crashing together as they fought, chasing the young fillies from other herds. The herdsmen rushed about in despair, chasing the fighting stallions, swearing at one another and sometimes even coming to blows, as they waved their whips. Gul'sary did not take part in all this. The sun shone between the showers, the grass was growing under the hooves. The meadows became the greenest of green and high above the snow shone white on the mountains. The dun pacer began to live through the most beautiful time of his life in that spring. From a long-coated dock-tailed foal of eighteen months, he was turning into a slender, strong young colt. He had grown; his body had lost its soft lines and was already getting a triangular form with broad breast and slender croup. His head was also becoming that of a true pacer, dry, hook-nosed with wide set eyes and gathered elastic lips. But he had no interest in growing up. Only one passion gripped him as yet—his passion for running. Leading on his rivals, he raced amongst them like some golden comet. Up the mountain slopes and down again, along the stony bank of the stream, up the steep paths along the hollows, an inexhaustible force drove him untiringly on. And even in the middle of the night when he slept under the stars, he dreamed how the earth would fly along under him, the wind whistling in his mane and ears, and his hooves clattering and ringing.

His feelings towards his master were like those towards anything else that did not directly affect him. He did not love him, but on the other hand he did not dislike him because his master did not as yet interfere in his life. Sometimes his master swore when he caught them up and they had gone too far away. Sometimes his master would hit him on the croup with the *ukruk*, the long stick with a noose on it with which he caught the horses. Gul'sary shivered then all over his body, but mainly because the blow was unexpected rather than because it hurt, and he would increase his speed. And the faster he ran on his way back to the herd, the happier was his master galloping along beside him with his *ukruk* across the saddle. Then the pacer heard behind him his master's shouts of approbation, heard how he began to sing as he rode and at those moments he loved his master and loved to race along to the song. Later he was to get to know these songs—they were many and varied, some happy, some sad, long and short, either with words to them or just tunes. He loved it, too, when

35

his master fed them salt. His master would throw the lumps of rock salt into the long wooden troughs on their supports. The whole herd fell on the salt; it was a real delight for the horses. And it was with the salt, too, that he was caught out.

One day his master was beating the empty bucket and calling the horses "Po, po, po!" The horses ran up and fell on the troughs. Gul'sary was licking the salt, standing amongst the others and was not at all alarmed when the master and his assistant began to move around the herd with their *ukruks*. This had never bothered him. They used to catch the milking mares and the riding horses with the *ukruks*, but never him. He was a free horse. And then suddenly the noose slipped over his head and down his neck. Gul'sary did not realise immediately what was happening, the noose did not alarm him yet and he went on licking the salt. The other horses had reared and pranced when they felt the noose, but Gul'sary did not stir. But suddenly he wanted to run down to the river to drink; he started away from the rest of the herd and then the noose tightened and stopped him. Nothing like this had ever happened to him before. Gul'sary recoiled, snorted, opened his eyes widely and reared up. The horses around him were off in a flash and there he was alone with the people holding him on the rough lasso. His master was nearest to him with the second herdsman just behind, and all around were the small sons of the herdsmen who had recently appeared on the scene and had already bored him with their antics as they rode around the herd.

Terror seized the pacer. He pranced again, again and again. The sunlight was flashing in his eyes and scattering in bright circles; the earth, the mountains, the people around were falling, and toppling over backwards. For a moment a frightening empty blackness covered his eyes and he struck out at it with his forelegs.

But however hard he struggled, the noose only got tighter and the choking pacer lunged not away from, but towards the people. The people dashed aside, the loop of the noose slackened and in his rush he dragged them across the ground. The women screamed and chased the boys over to the *yurtas*. However, the herdsmen got to their feet and the noose tightened once more on Gul'sary's back. This time it was so tight that he just could not breathe. So with his head swimming he stood still and helpless, half strangled.

Taking up the slack of the lasso, his master started to approach from one side; Gul'sary watched him with one eye. His master (with the scars on his face) came up to him in his shabby torn clothes. But his master's eyes looked at him without malice. He was breathing heavily, clucking with his battered lips, and quietly, almost in a whisper he said:

"Tek, tek, Gul'sary, don't be frightened, stand, stand!" His assistant came carefully up from behind without loosening the halter, at last, his master stretched out his hand to the pacer, stroked his head and said shortly, without turning round:

"Head collar."

The other handed him the head collar.

"Hold, Gul'sary, stand, you wise horse," said his master. He covered the pacer's eyes with his arm as he slipped the collar over his head.

Now he had to fully bridle and saddle him. When the bridle was put over his head, Gul'sary snorted and tried to break away. But his master seized him by the upper lip.

"Twitch!" he shouted to his helper who ran up, quickly put the twitch on the lip and started to twist it with the stick, as if with a capstan.

The pacer fell down on his hind legs with the pain and resisted no more. The cold steel of the bit scraped on his teeth and stuck into the corners of his mouth. Someone threw something on his back and tightened it up, and with quick pulls secured straps round his breast so that he rocked from side to side. But this was nothing compared with this overwhelming senseless pain in his lip. His eyes stared. He could not move at all nor breathe. And he did not even notice when his master mounted him, but only came to himself when they took off the twitch from his lips.

He stood for a minute or two, heavy and constricted, then he looked over his shoulder and suddenly caught sight of the man on his back. In his fright he tried to lurch forward but the bit tore at his mouth, and the man's legs gripped his sides firmly. The dun pranced, neighed in anger and fury, tried to rush away, kicked out with his hind legs and longed to throw the man and everything else off his back. He lurched sideways, but the halter, secured by the man on another horse, held him fast. So he tried to run around in a circle, hoping as he ran to break away and race off wherever his fancy took him. But he could not break loose and had to go on running round and round. This was just what the people wanted. His master whipped him and dug into his flanks with his heels. Twice the pacer succeeded in throwing him but each time his master remounted.

This went on for a long, long time. His head was still swimming, the earth and the *yurtas* were revolving around him, swirling with the horses in the distance and the mountains and the clouds in the sky. Later he tired and began to walk. How he wanted a drink.

But they did not give him a drink. That evening they did not unsaddle him, but merely loosened the girth and tied him up by the pickets where they rested the horses. The reins were tied to the pommel so that he had to hold his head straight and level; he just could not lie down.

The stirrups were run up and laid across the saddle. Thus he stood all night. He stood obediently, broken by all the unbelievable things that had happened and which he must endure. The bit in his mouth was nagging, the slightest movement caused him pain and he was disgusted by the taste of the iron. The swollen corners of his mouth were stretched. There was a pain on his flank where the straps had rubbed. Under the saddle cloth his back was aching. How he wanted a drink! He could hear the noise of the stream and this made his thirst even worse. There beyond the stream as always, the herds were grazing. He could hear the sound of many hooves, neighing and the distant shouts of the night herdsmen. People sat near the *yurtas* by the fires and rested. The boys were teasing the dogs by imitating their yelping. He just stood there and no one came or took any notice of him.

Then the moon came out. The mountains quietly appeared out of the haze and seemed to be gently swaying, lit up in the light of the yellow moon ... The stars shone brighter as if dipping closer to the earth. As he stood still, tethered to the same spot, someone was about looking for him. He heard the whinnying of the small bay filly with whom he had grown up and from whom he was inseparable. She had a white star on her forehead and loved to run with him. Already the young stallions were starting to chase her but she would not let them get near; she ran away from them with him. She was still too young for them and he was not old enough to do what the other stallions tried to do.

Now there was a whinny close at hand. Yes, it was she; he knew her voice so well. He wanted to answer her, but was afraid to open his swollen, strained mouth. It was so painful. At last she found him. She came up with her easy movement, her star shining in the moonlight. Her tail and legs were wet. She had come across the river bringing with her the cool smell of the water. She touched him with her nose, began to sniff him and then caressed him with her warm, soft, mobile lips. She neighed gently, calling him to come with her and away. But he could not move at all. Then she rested her head on his neck and began to comb through his mane with her teeth. He too would have liked to rest his head on her neck and rub her withers; but he could not move. He wanted to drink, if only she could bring him water! When she ran off, he gazed after her, following her until her shadow dissolved in the twilight across the stream. She had come to him and gone away. The tears flowed from his eyes, down his face in big drops and noiselessly fell at his hooves. The pacer was weeping for the first time in his life.

Early in the morning his master came. He looked around at the mountains in their spring loveliness; he stretched and smiled and groaned with his stiffness.

"Gul'sary, what a time you gave me yesterday! Eh? You're cold? What a state you got into."

He patted the pacer on the neck and said something that seemed kind and funny to him. How was Gul'sary to understand? But Tanabai said, "Don't be angry, my friend. You cannot spend your whole life wandering around doing nothing. You'll get used to work, it'll be all right. I know what you suffered but you can't avoid that. Life, brother, is what puts the shoes on your four hooves. But later on you will not shy at every stone on the road. You're hungry? Want a drink? I understand."

He led the pacer down to the stream. He took off the harness and removed the bit from his sore mouth. Gul'sary shivered as he

39

touched the water with his lips. The cold struck right through to his eyes. But how tasty the water was and how grateful he was to the man for this drink.

That's how it had been. Soon he got so used to the saddle that he felt no more discomfort. He carried a rider easily and happily. His master always had to hold him back, but still he raced on, leaving on the track the accurate mark of his pacing gait. He learnt to move with the saddle on so swiftly and smoothly that the people watching would gasp, "Put a bucket of water on his back and he wouldn't spill a drop!"

And when Tanabai took him to show to the old herdsman, Torgoi said:

"Thank you; you've schooled him well. Now you will see the star of your pacer climb up in the sky."

3

The wheels of the old cart slowly scraped their way over the desert road. From time to time the scraping ceased when the pacer stopped exhausted. Then in the deathly silence he could hear in his ears the dull beats of his own heart, toom-toop, toom-toop, toom-toop.

Old Tanabai waited for the horse to regather strength before picking up the reins once more.

"Come on, Gul'sary, come on; it's evening already."

In this way they struggled on for an hour and a half until the pacer stopped altogether. He just could not drag the cart any further. Tanabai got down again and began to fuss round the horse.

"What's up now, Gul'sary, eh? Look, it's night already."

But the horse did not understand him! He stood between the shafts, his enormously heavy head hanging, staggering from side to side and the heart beats thudding in his ears.

"Oh, forgive me," said Tanabai, "I should have guessed earlier. The devil take the cart and the harness, let's get you home."

He flung his coat to the ground and quickly got to work unharnessing the horse. He took him from the shafts, removed his collar and threw all the harness into the cart.

"That's the lot," he said and as he struggled back into his coat he looked at the unharnessed horse. Without the harness, with his enormous head, the horse stood there in the evening cold of the steppe like a ghost.

"Oh God, what has become of you, Gul'sary?" whispered Tanabai, "If Torgoi could see you now he'd turn over in his grave . . ."

He pulled at the pacer with the halter and they began to wander along the road again. Old horse and old man. Behind them lay the abandoned cart and ahead in the west was the dark

41

purple night over the road. The night had descended quietly over the steppe, obscuring the mountains and obliterating the horizon.

As Tanabai walked he remembered everything connected with the pacer over the long years and thought with bitter amusement about people in general: "We're all the same. We remember one another at the end of life when someone is seriously ill or dying. Then everything suddenly becomes clear to us; the man we have lost, what sort of a person he was, what he was famous for and what he achieved. And what about dumb animals? Who has not ridden on Gul'sary? What efforts he made and now everyone has forgotten about him. Here he is struggling on his way, scarcely able to drag himself along. But what a horse he was in his day!"

Once again he thought about the past and was surprised that he had not turned his thoughts back for so long. Everything seemed to come alive again. Nothing was entirely lost. Earlier he had thought little about his past, or more truthfully had not let himself think about it. But now, after the words with his son and his daughter-in-law, as he walked along the road in the night leading his dying horse, he looked back with pain and sadness over the past years as they unrolled before him.

Thus he struggled on deep in his thoughts, and the pacer dragged on behind, pulling more and more at the halter. When the old man's hand became numb, he changed over to the other hand and shoulder. But this was uncomfortable and he stopped to give them both a rest. He considered things for a bit and then took the halter off the horse.

"You go in front. Do the best you can and I will walk behind you, I won't desert you," he said, "Come on now, take it gently."

Thus they went on with Tanabai behind carrying the halter over his shoulder. He would not throw away the head collar. Whenever Gul'sary stopped, Tanabai waited until he had regained some strength and then they went on again. Old horse and old man.

Tanabai smiled gloomily as he recalled that it was along this very road that Gul'sary, in his prime, used to run with a cloud of dust like a long tail stretching behind him. The shepherds used to

42

say that with one look at the dust cloud they could tell from many *versty* away that Gul'sary was coming. The dust raised by his hooves flew out over the steppe in a growing white cloud and in calm weather it lay over the road like the condensation trail from a high-flying jet. A shepherd would stand there shading his eyes, and say, "There goes Gul'sary." And with a pang of envy he would think about the lucky person, face scorched by the hot wind, who was flying along on this horse. It was a great honour for a Kirgiz to ride on such a famous pacer.

Gul'sary lived to see many presidents at the *kolkhoz*, honest and dishonest, some clever ones, some born fools, but all used to ride Gul'sary from the first day of their taking office to the last.

"Where are they now? Do they ever remember Gul'sary who carried them on his back from dawn to dusk?" thought Tanabai.

At long last they reached the bridge over the river and stopped again.

The pacer started to bend his legs in order to lie down. Tanabai could not let him do that for once down, no power on earth would get him up again.

"Stand up, stand up," he shouted and struck the horse's head with the halter. At once he felt deep shame for striking the blow, but continued to shout, "Don't you understand? Do you want to die? I won't let you! You must not! Get up! Get up! Get up!" He dragged the horse up by the mane.

Gul'sary straightened his legs with difficulty and gave a deep groan. Although it was dark, Tanabai did not dare to glance towards the horse's eyes. He stroked him, felt him and then put his head against the left flank. There in the horse's chest he could hear the heart straining, beating like a mill-wheel against water plants. He stood there bending down beside the horse until his back ached. Then he straightened up, shook his head and sighed; he had decided that a risk would have to be taken. He would turn off the road just past the bridge, on to the path which ran beside the ravine. The path by which they would get home quicker led into the mountains. It would be easy to get lost at night, but Tanabai felt sure of himself, he had known the track for many years; if only the horse could last out.

While the old man considered this plan, the lights of a lorry

43

appeared behind them, far away in the distance. They had suddenly appeared from the mist like two bright circles of fire and were approaching quickly, feeling their way along the road with the rays extending like feelers in front. Tanabai and Gul'sary stood by the bridge. The vehicle could not help them in any way, but all the same Tanabai waited for it. "At last someone is coming," he thought. Just the idea that there were people on the road gave him some comfort. The glare of the headlights suddenly fell on his eyes and he had to shadow them with his hand.

The two men in the cab of the lorry looked out with amazement at the old man by the bridge with the gaunt nag beside him, with no saddle or harness just like a dog clinging to its master. For an instant the direct glare lit up the old man and his horse and turned them into white, ghostly shapes.

"What on earth is he doing here in the middle of the night?" said the lanky youth in the fur cap.

"That must have been his cart back there," explained the driver and stopped. "What's wrong, old man?" he shouted as he leaned out of the cab. "Was that your cart back there?"

"Yes, that's mine," said Tanabai.

"Ah well. We saw the old wreck by the roadside. No one near it. We thought about taking the harness, but that was useless as well."

Tanabai was silent.

The driver climbed out, walked the few paces and breathed a stale, heavy smell of vodka over the old man. He began to piss on the road.

"What happened to you, then?" he asked over his shoulder.

"My horse couldn't draw the cart any further. He's ill . . . and he's old."

"Mm. Where are you making for now?"

"Home . . . to the Sarygousk ravine."

"Phew!" whistled the driver, "Up in the mountains? It's not on our way. But climb in the cab, sit with us and we'll put you out at the State farm and you can get a lift on from there tomorrow."

"No, thank you. I've got the horse."

"What, this bag of bones? Go on, leave it to the dogs, push it

44

over into the ravine . . . that'll be the end and the crows can peck it. Like us to help you?"

"Go on your way!" Tanabai gloomily forced the words out.

"Huh, you know best." The driver smiled ironically and slamming the door of the lorry, he called to his companion, "The old man's half mad!"

The lorry moved off, taking with it the dim dust-obscured pool of light. The bridge over the ravine creaked in the light of the brake-lights.

"Why did you laugh at the old chap? What if something like that happened to you one day?" said the young man in the cab.

"Nonsense," the driver yawned as he twisted the wheel, "I've had to do lots of things like that in my time. I was talking sense. Just think of that wretched old horse. A thing of the past. Now, brother, technology is the thing. Everywhere machinery is taking over, even for war. It's the end of the road for such old men and their horses."

"You're a heartless beast," said the youth.

"I don't give a damn," said the driver.

When the lorry had gone, and the night had closed in around them once more and when their eyes had got used to the dark again, Tanabai urged on the pacer.

"Off we go! Chu, chu. On you go."

Past the bridge he turned the horse off the main road on to the track. Now they moved slowly along the path, which was scarcely visible in the darkness over the ravine. The moon was just beginning to rise over the mountains and the stars, waiting its arrival, were twinkling coldly in the bleak sky.

4

Late in the same year that Gul'sary was broken in and schooled the herds were taken from the autumn pasture. It was a longer autumn than usual and the winter was mild; the frequent snow did not settle and there was plenty to eat. In the spring the herds came down to the foothills again and, as soon as the steppe began to break into flower, they moved down there.

After the war, this was perhaps the best time in Tanabai's life. The grey horse of old age, though not far off, was still waiting for him over the hill, and Tanabai was still riding the young dun pacer. If this pacer had come into his life and hands some few years later, he would scarcely have experienced such joy, such virile excitement as riding Gul'sary gave him. Yes, Tanabai was not past showing off in front of people. And how could he avoid doing so, when he rode such a magnificent pacer! Gul'sary was well aware of this—especially when Tanabai was riding to the village across the field where he used to catch up with the women walking in a party to their work. Even some way from them, he tensely drew himself up in the saddle and his excitement was transmitted to the horse. Gul'sary raised his tail so that it was almost in line with his back and his mane flattened and whistled in the breeze. Snorting, he zigzagged slightly, carrying his rider easily. The women in their white and red scarves ran to the sides of the road, up to their knees in the young green corn. They stopped there as if bewitched then suddenly turned towards him, with their faces, shining eyes, smiles and white teeth flashing.

"Hi, herdsman! Stop!" The cries flew after him, as he passed. "Look out! If you fall off, we'll catch you!"

And sometimes they did indeed catch him, blocking his path with joined hands. Women love to play the fool! Dragging Tanabai from the saddle they laughed, squealed, and snatched the whip from his hands.

"When will you bring us some *kumys*? We're here every day

working from morning to evening while you ride around on your pacer."

"What's stopping you? Come and work as herdswomen. Only tell your husbands that they'd better look out for some other girls. You'll freeze like icicles up in the mountains."

"Oh, is that how it is?" and they began to pester him again.

But Tanabai never once let anyone sit on his pacer. Not even that woman who could change his mood completely when he met her, and then he would make the pacer break into a walk. Not even she ever rode once on his horse. Perhaps she did not wish to.

That year Tanabai was appointed to the inspection committee. Often he rode to the village and practically every time he would meet this woman. He had often left the office in a temper. Gul'sary felt this from his eyes, his voice, the movements of his hands. But as soon as he met her, Tanabai always became kinder.

"Whoa, there. Quietly now, where are you racing off to like that?" he whispered, calming the high-spirited pacer and as he came level with her he broke into a walk.

Sometimes they would talk quietly and sometimes they were just silent together. Gul'sary felt the cares falling away from his master, his voice becoming gentle and warm and his hands more caressing. Therefore he loved to meet this woman on their way.

How was the horse to know that life in the *kolkhoz* was tough, that they got precious little in return for their work but inspection-committee member Tanabai closely questioned those in the office to try and find out why? When in the future would life begin in which there would not only be something to give to the State, but something for themselves too?

Last year the crops had failed and there had been a dearth of fodder. This year they had had to give grain and cattle, over and above the plan, to others so that the region would not fall on its face in the mud. What could the members of the *kolkhoz* count on—they just did not know. Time had passed, they had already begun to forget the war, but they lived in the same way—on what they could squeeze out of their own plots and on what they could glean in the fields. There were no funds in the *kolkhoz*; everything was handed over at a loss, milk, grain, and meat. In the

47

summer the animals bred well and flourished, but in the winter there was tragedy when the animals died from hunger and cold. They had to build stables, cowsheds and storage for the fodder, but they could get no materials anywhere and no one would promise to give them any. What had happened, too, about housing after the war? Only the private cattle and potato traders did any building. Because of their increasing influence, they were the only ones able to pick up the necessary building materials.

"No, it shouldn't be like this, comrades, something is wrong; we have a big difficulty here," said Tanabai, "I do not believe things should be like this. Either we have forgotten how to work or you are directing us wrongly."

"What is wrong? What is incorrect?" The accountant pushed papers in front of him. "Look at the plans ... this is what we received, this is what we have paid out, here's the debit, here's the credit side, here's the balance. No profit, only loss. What more do you want? Work it out from the start. Are you the only communist and the rest of us enemies of the people, eh?"

Others joined in the discussion, a noisy argument started, and Tanabai sat there, his head in his hands and thought in despair —what on earth is happening? He suffered for the *kolkhoz*, not only because he worked in it—but for other, special reasons. There were people who had old scores to settle with Tanabai. He knew that they were laughing at him now and that when they saw him they looked challengingly as if to say, "Well and how are things now? Perhaps you want to start throwing out the *kulaks* again? But we have a little request that you get down off your high horse. Why didn't you get your packet at the front?"

And he looked back at them with the reply: "Wait, you scum, we'll get everything we want in the end." But these were his own people. His step-brother Kulubai was now an old man and had done his seven years in Siberia before the war. His sons have taken after him, and hate Tanabai fiercely. Why should they love him? Perhaps their children will also hate Tanabai's family. They have good reason to. All that happened long ago, but the resentment lives on. How would he have acted in Kulubai's case? Was he not just a manager, a middle peasant? What about the family tie? Kulubai was the son of the elder wife and he the son

48

of the younger; but the Kirgiz consider such brothers as from the same womb. In other words he had acted against his family and there were many disputes then about the case. Now, of course, one can look at things differently. But then? He had done what he did for the sake of the *kolkhoz*, hadn't he? And it had all been necessary? Earlier he had had no doubt about his duty, but after the war he had sometimes had second thoughts. Hadn't he made many unnecessary enemies in the *kolkhoz*?

"Come on, Tanabai, what are you sitting there for? Wake up!" Thus they brought him back to the discussion. It was the same old business again; first they have to collect all the manure together in the yards, then cart it out to the fields after the winter. There is a shortage of serviceable cart wheels so they have to buy *karagach* wood and iron for the rims. But what about the necessary money? Would they give them credit? The bank needs more than words as security. Then it is necessary to repair the old irrigation ditches, dig new ones—a big programme of heavy work. The people cannot go out to do that in winter, the ground is frozen solid and cannot be broken. In the spring it is too late, there is the sowing, the lambing, weeding and then the hay-making. What about the sheep? Where are the breeding pens? And on the dairy side are things any better? The roof is rotting, there's not enough fodder, the milkmaids don't want to get on with their work. They play around from morning to night and what is the result? And how many more problems and insufficiencies are there? Sometimes it is just awful to think about it all.

But all the same there was no apathy. Again they discussed these questions at the party meeting and in the *kolkhoz* management. Choro was then the president. Only later on did Tanabai appreciate his worth. It was easier, it seemed, to criticise. Tanabai was responsible just for the herd of horses, but Choro had to answer for everyone and everything on the *kolkhoz*. Yes, Choro was a tower of strength. When it seemed that everything was collapsing around them, when they beat their fists on the table at him in the region centre or seized him by the coat collar out on the farm, Choro was not put out at all. In his shoes Tanabai would have gone off his head or done away with himself. But Choro kept his farm going and stood firm to the end until his heart gave up—but even then he served for another two years as party affairs organiser. Choro knew how to convince, how to speak to people. Having heard Choro speak even Tanabai could once again believe that all would be sorted out and in the end they would achieve what they had dreamed about in the early days. Only once was his faith in Choro shaken, but even then that was more his own fault.

The pacer did not know what was going on inside Tanabai when he walked out of the office with an angry look and knitted brows, and pitched himself roughly into the saddle pulling harshly on the reins. He felt that things were very bad for his master and although Tanabai had never struck him, he feared his master in those minutes. But once he saw that woman ahead on the road, the horse sensed at once that it would be easier for his master. He would become kind again and make Gul'sary break into a walk, and would talk quietly with her about something and her hands would pat Gul'sary, stroke his mane and neck. No other person had such caressing hands. They were wonderful hands, soft and gentle like the lips of that little bay filly with the star on her forehead. And no one on earth had eyes like that woman. Tanabai talked with her, bending down from the saddle and she would smile or frown, shake her head when she disagreed and her eyes would be filled with either light or shade, like the stones on the bed of a fast-flowing stream in the moonlight. As she walked away, she would turn and again shake her head.

After this Tanabai would ride on in deep thought. He let the reins go slack and Gul'sary walked on freely, then at a trot. It was as if his master was not in the saddle, just as if he and horse were separate beings. And the song would begin, also separate. Quietly, not clearly, in time with the movement of the pacer, Tanabai sang about the sufferings of people long ago. And the horse would make his way along the track he had chosen, carrying his master to the steppe across the river to the herds ...

Gul'sary loved it when his master was in this mood; and he loved this woman too in his own way. He knew her figure, her walk, he noticed even the strong wild smell of some grass or herb unknown to him. It was clove. She wore beads of clove.

"See how he loves you, Byubyuzhan," said Tanabai. "Go on,

stroke him, stroke him again. Look how his ears are flattened back. He's just like a calf. But he does not give the herd up there much peace. Just let him go and he snaps at the stallions like a dog. That's why I keep him for riding, I'm afraid they might injure him. He's green yet."

"Yes, he does love me," she mused to herself.

"Meaning, others don't?"

"I'm not talking about that. The time for our love has passed. I shall be sorry for you."

"Why, indeed?"

"You're not that sort of person, it will be hard for you later on."

"But for you?"

"What do I matter? I'm a widow, a soldier's widow. But you . . ."

"I'm a member of the inspection committee. I met you and I am explaining certain facts to you," Tanabai tried to make a joke of it.

"Somehow you have begun to explain facts rather often. Think about it."

"Uh, but where do I come into it? You are walking and I am walking, too."

"I'm going my way. We cannot go the same way. Ah well, good-bye. I've no time now."

"Listen, Byubyuzhan!"

"Now what? No need, Tanabai. Why? You are no fool. I'm miserable enough without you adding to it."

"What, am I your enemy?"

"You're your own enemy."

"How should I take that?"

"As you wish."

She went on her way and Tanabai rode about the streets of the settlement, as if he was doing some errands. He went up to the mill, looked in at the school and came back in a circle. He returned in order to watch from afar as she left her mother-in-law's house, where she left her daughter whilst she was at work and when she returned to her home on the edge of the village, leading her daughter by the hand. Everything about her was eternally dear to him, the way she walked, trying not to look in his direction, with her white face framed in her dark shawl and her little daughter and the little dog running with them.

At last she disappeared and he went on his way, imagining to himself how she would open the door of the empty house and put on her old jacket or run out for water and light the fire. Then she would wash and feed the child and go to meet her cow as it came down with the others. At night she would lie by herself in the dark, silent house and would persuade herself, and hence him, that they must not love one another, that he was a man with a family, that at his age it was ridiculous to fall in love, that everything has its time, that his wife was a fine woman and her husband should not want another.

Such thoughts made Tanabai sick at heart. "It just is not my fate." As he thought, he looked into the misty distance across the river and began to sing his old songs, forgetting about everything in the world, about his work, the *kolkhoz*, the shoes and the clothes for the children, about friends and enemies and about his step-brother Kulubai, to whom he had not spoken for many years. He forgot about the war, about which he occasionally dreamed, to wake in a cold sweat; he forgot about everything in his life. He did not notice that the horse had forded the river, and coming out on the far side was continuing on his way. He only came back to reality when the pacer, responding to the nearness of the herd, began to go faster.

"Steady, Gul'sary, what's the hurry?" he stuttered, pulling on the reins.

5

In spite of everything it was a wonderful time for him and Gul'sary. The fame of a horse is rather like that of a footballer. The small boy of yesterday, kicking a ball around the backyard, suddenly becomes everyone's favourite, a subject of endless discussion for the fans and the delight of the crowd. His fame will grow more and more, so long as he scores goals. Then he gradually disappears from the scene and is entirely forgotten. Those who forget quickest are those who were the most vociferous. So the great footballer gives place to another. Fame is the same for a horse. He is well-known as long as he wins. The only difference, indeed, is that no one envies a horse. Horses do not know how to envy and people, thank God, have not yet learnt to envy horses. But the ways of envy are incomprehensible; cases are known for the envious to drive a nail into the hoof of their enemy's horse. That is the blackest envy! . . . But leave that for God . . .

The prophecy of the old man Torgoi came true. That spring the star of the pacer rose high. Everyone knew about him, old and young alike. "Gul'sary", "Tanabai's pacer", "The pride of the village".

Dirty-faced little boys, not able yet to sound their "r's", ran about the dusty street, copying the pacer and shouting one to the other, "I'm Gul'saly" . . . "No, I'm Gul'saly" . . . "Mama, say that I'm Gul'saly . . . from now on, ai-ai, I'm Gul'saly!"

What fame is and what strength it gives, the pacer was yet to find out on his first big race meeting. That was to be on the first of May.

After a meeting in the big meadow by the river, the games began. People had walked and ridden in from miles around. Some had come from the next *kolkhoz*, down from the mountains and some even from Kazakhstan. The Kazakhs were showing their horses. People said that there had not been such a big show since the war.

Early in the morning, when Tanabai saddled him and checked the girths and the stirrup leathers with special care, the pacer could see from his master's shining eyes and shaky hands that something unusual was about to happen. His master was indeed very excited.

"Now Gul'sary, don't you let us down," he whispered, as he combed out the horse's mane and fore-lock. "You must not shame us, do you hear? We've no right to allow that."

The expectation in the air could be felt in the excited voices and the bustling throng. The herdsmen were saddling their horses at the various stables near by. Small boys were already shouting as they rode around on their horses. Then all the herdsmen joined up in a party and moved off towards the river.

Gul'sary was most surprised by such a vast collection of people and horses on the meadow. Noise and hubbub were everywhere, by the river, on the meadow and amongst the hillocks along the water meadows. The bright scarves and dresses, the red flags and the white turbans of the women dazzled the eyes. The horses were all in their best tackle; stirrup irons rang, bridles and the silver pendants on the breast-plates rattled.

The horses with their riders were crowded together in rows, were impatiently stamping, asking to walk around and digging at the ground with their hooves. In the ring the old men, the officials of the games, were prancing about.

Gul'sary could feel the excitement growing inside him and a latent strength filling his being. It seemed to him that some fiery spirit had moved into him and in order to free himself, he would have to break into the ring and race around it.

When the officials gave the signal for him to go into the ring, Tanabai eased the reins and the pacer advanced to the centre and turned around not knowing where to go. Along the ranks of the spectators went the cry "Gul'sary, Gul'sary!"

All who wished to take part in the great *baiga* or contest had come into the ring. There were some fifty horses and riders.

"Ask for the blessing of the people," proclaimed the chief judge solemnly.

The riders with their shaven heads and the tight bands around their foreheads, rode along the lines of the spectators with open hands and from end to end of the line came the united cry of "O-

O-miin" and hundreds of hands were raised to foreheads and were lowered over the faces like flowing streams of water.

After this the riders trotted off to the starting place some nine kilometres away. During this time other games were started in the arena—fights between mounted men and men on foot. There were contests in which men were dragged from the saddle and riders picked up money from the ground. But this was only a diversion, the main event was beginning over by the starting point.

Gul'sary got very restless on the way there. He did not understand why his master held him in check. All around other horses were prancing and excited because there were so many of them all asking to be given their heads. The pacer was also on edge and shivered with impatience.

At last they were all lined up, head to head, and the starter rode across the line; at the end he raised the white flag. Everyone froze on their marks, excited and expectant. The flag waved. The horses streamed forward and in the first impetuous rush Gul'sary was right up with them, racing ahead. The earth shook under the pounding hooves and the dust rose high. The horses broke into a full gallop to the accompaniment of the whooping and shouts of their riders. Only Gul'sary, who could not gallop, continued with his pacing action. In this lay both his weakness and his strength.

At first all were bunched together, but after only a few moments the field began to open out. Gul'sary did not see this. He only saw that the fast, racing horses had passed him and were already drawing ahead. Their hooves threw up stones and lumps of dry mud over him and all around were horses, shouting riders, whistling whips and clouds of dust. The dust formed a great cloud rising over the earth. There was a strong mingled smell of sweat, flint sparks and young crushed wormwood.

Thus they continued almost to the half-way mark. Out ahead raced some ten horses at a speed unattainable for a pacer. On either side it was quiet and the sound of the stragglers was lost behind. But the fact that there were others in front, that the reins were holding him back and not giving him full freedom roused the fury in him.

His rage and the wind in his eyes darkened his sight, the track passed rapidly beneath him and the sun raced towards him like a ball of fire. He was covered in hot sweat and the more he sweated the easier it was for him to run.

Then came the moment when the fast racers began to tire and gradually drop back, losing speed; but the pacer was just reaching his peak. "Chu, Gul'sary, chu," he heard his master's voice. The sun came more quickly towards him. One by one the faces of the riders, distorted with anger, were passed and left behind, as were the slashing whips and the grunting mouths of the horses. Suddenly the drag of bit and rein vanished. It seemed to Gul'sary that there was neither saddle nor rider on his back only deep inside him the burning passion of the race.

Still in front there were two horses left, racing neck and neck, a dark grey and a chestnut. Driven on by their riders' shouts and whips, neither gave an inch. These were real stayers. Gul'sary took a long time to catch them up but as they came up a slope, he drew ahead at last. He came to the top of the rise, as if on a crest of a vast wave and for a moment he seemed to fly, weightless. It took his breath away and the sun shone even brighter in his eyes; then he raced away downhill on the other side but soon heard the sound of hooves behind. These two, the dark grey and the chestnut, were now out for revenge; they came up on both flanks together and showed no signs of giving ground.

Thus the three raced, neck and neck, almost as one. It seemed to Gul'sary that they were no longer moving, but had simply frozen in a strange torpidity and silence. He could even see the expression in the eye of the horse next to him, the straining of the mouths, the chewed bits, bridles and reins. The dark grey looked obstinate and fierce, but the chestnut looked worried and his gaze was wandering. It was he in fact who first began to fall back. First his ashamed and wandering gaze, then his nose with the wide nostrils and then he himself disappeared. But the dark grey held on for an agonisingly long time. He was slowly dying as he ran, his expression gradually becoming glassy from impotent rage; then at last he fell back, still unwilling to acknowledge his defeat.

When Gul'sary's rivals left him it was easier to breathe. Ahead was the stream shining silver and the green meadow and the distant roar of voices. The most enthusiastic spectators were waiting on horseback out on the trackside. With hallooing and whooping they rode alongside. Suddenly Gul'sary felt the onset of weakness and the distance telling. Gul'sary did not know what was going on behind, whether they would catch him or not. It became almost impossible to run on, his strength was leaving him.

But then ahead of him the great crowd roared and swayed and already the two lines of spectators, both on horse and on foot, were coming up like a vast sleeve; the shouting became louder and stronger. Suddenly, distinctly, he heard "Gul'sary! Gul'sary! Gul'sary!" and these shouts he gathered in, these cries and yells, they filled him as if with fresh air and he raced down with new strength. Oh, people, people! There is nothing that they cannot do . . . !

Gul'sary raced through this booming corridor of people to the accompaniment of an unceasing roar of shouts and excitement and then, easing up, he circled round the meadow.

But it was not all over. For now neither he nor his master were their own. When the pacer had got his breath back and had calmed down a little and the people had edged away forming a circle around him, then again the cries rang out "Gul'sary! Gul'sary! Gul'sary!" and at the same time they shouted for his master, "Tanabai! Tanabai! Tanabai!"

Once again the people achieved a miracle and gave Gul'sary new strength. Proudly and impetuously he entered the arena with his head high and blazing eyes. Drunk with his triumph, Gul'sary began to dance. He walked sideways and broke into a new step. He knew that he was beautiful, powerful and famous.

Tanabai rode round the spectators with his hands stretched out as a conqueror and again from all sides there rose the sound of the words of the people's blessing "O-O-miin" and once more hundreds of hands were raised to foreheads and were lowered over the faces like flowing streams of water.

Suddenly amongst the multitude of people Gul'sary saw that woman he knew. He recognised her at once when her hand moved over her face, although this time she was not wearing her dark shawl, but a white scarf. She stood in the front row of the crowd, happy and joyful, her gaze fixed on them with those shining eyes like stones in a fast flowing stream. Out of habit Gul'sary moved towards her so that his master could talk with her and she could finger his mane and stroke his neck with her wonderful hands, soft and gentle like the lips of that little bay filly with the star on her forehead. But Tanabai for some reason tightened the reins and pulled him away. The pacer tried to turn to go to her again, not understanding what his master was doing. Surely his master could see that here was the woman whom he had to talk to?

On the next day, the second of May, Gul'sary had another triumph. In the afternoon they played the steppe game of goat snatching—a sort of mounted football, in which instead of a ball, the headless carcase of a goat is used. The goat is convenient for this as its hair is long and strong and can be picked up from the saddle by the leg or the skin.

Again the steppe rang with the traditional shouts, again the earth sounded like a drum. The avalanche of mounted fans milled around the players with cries and yells. Once again Gul'sary was the hero of the day. On this occasion having already earned his crown of glory, he was immediately the most important figure in the game. Tanabai, however, was holding him in check for the final stage, for the *alaman-baiga*, when the players were permitted to have a free-for-all and the quickest and most skilful then took the goat off to his village as the victor. Everyone was waiting for the *alaman-baiga*, because this was the climax of the contest and every rider present had the right to take part in it and everyone wanted to try his luck.

The May sun was already lying low over the distant Kazakhstan side. It was yellow, swollen and covered with a light cloud. One could look at it without blinking.

Right up to the evening the Kirgiz and the Kazakhs raced around, leaning from their saddles and snatching up the goat at the gallop, tearing it from each other, gathering into a shouting scrum and then breaking away again and noisily racing over the field.

And only when the long broken shadows began to lengthen over the steppe did the elders decide that the time for the *alaman-baiga* had come. The goat was thrown into the circle and the cry went up *"Alaman!"*

The riders raced in from every side, crowding in, trying to

snatch the carcase from the ground. But in the mêlée this was not so simple. The horses raced around crazily, bit one another and bared their teeth. Gul'sary fell back in this struggle, his place was out in the open so Tanabai just could not get his hands on the goat. Suddenly a piercing shout rang out, "Look out, the Kazakhs have got it!" Out of the maelstrom of horses a young Kazakh in a torn tunic broke loose on a wild brown stallion. He raced away dragging the carcase of the goat under his stirrup iron.

"Look out! The brown!" everyone shouted, as all raced in pursuit, "Faster, Tanabai, only you can catch him!"

With the goat dangling under his stirrup, the Kazakh on the brown stallion was away directly towards the bright setting sun. It seemed as if any moment he would fly off into the sun and be consumed in red smoke.

Gul'sary did not understand why Tanabai was holding him in check, but Tanabai knew that first he had to let the Kazakh break loose from the milling mass and get separated from his fellows racing to help him. They only had to surround the brown horse with a galloping escort and then it would be impossible to snatch away the trophy. Only in single combat could Tanabai count on success.

Having waited as long as was necessary, Tanabai then gave the pacer his head at full strength. Gul'sary nestled close to the ground, racing towards the approaching sun as the noise and shouts behind him began to drop away, further and further, and the distance to the brown stallion began to close. The brown was heavily laden and it was not difficult to catch him. Tanabai came up on the right-hand side where the carcase was pressed tightly under the rider's leg. Now they were level and Tanabai leant over to snatch the goat by the leg and drag it over to him. But the Kazakh skilfully changed the trophy over to his left side while his horse raced on towards the sun. Tanabai first had to drop back and then catch up again on the other side. It was difficult to get the pacer to give any ground, but all the same he succeeded. Once again the Kazakh with the torn tunic managed to change the goat over.

"Good man!" shouted Tanabai in his excitement.

The horses raced on towards the sun. There was no time to be lost or to take any chances. Tanabai pressed right up against the brown and lay across the pommel of his neighbour's saddle. The Kazakh tried to break away but Tanabai would not let him. The speed and versatility of the pacer allowed him to lie almost on the neck of the brown horse. In this way he reached out for and seized the carcase and began to pull it over. He could do this more easily from this side as both his hands were free. He had already got the carcase half-way across.

"You've had it, brother Kazakh," shouted Tanabai.

"You lie. I won't let it go," came the answer.

As they rode madly on a fierce struggle broke out. As they grappled like eagles over the same prey, they swore hoarse obscenities, grunting like animals, each trying to scare the other. Hands were interlocked, blood flowed from under their nails. The horses linked together by the single combat of their riders raced on enraged, trying to catch up with the blood-red sun.

May our ancestors be blessed for handing down to us these manly contests for the brave!

The goat carcase was now between them and they were sharing its weight in the space between their horses. The moment of decision was near. Silent, teeth clenched, they exerted all their strength as they dragged on the goat, each trying to get it under his leg and to break away from his rival. The Kazakh was strong; his hands were large and sinewy and he was much younger than Tanabai. But experience counts. Tanabai unexpectedly took his right foot out of the stirrup iron and pushed it into the side of the brown stallion. As he dragged the goat over, he simultaneously gave his rival's horse a further shove with his leg and saw his hands slip.

"Look out!" his victim managed to shout a warning.

From the sharp reaction as they split apart Tanabai nearly fell from his saddle, but just managed to hold on. With a great yell of triumph he turned the pacer away and made off. He pressed the honourably gained trophy under his stirrup leather. The horde of yelling riders galloped up towards them.

"Gul'sary has got it! Gul'sary has it!"

A large group of Kazakhs were trying to intercept him.

"*Oi-bai*, catch and hold Tanabai!"

Now the main thing was to escape capture and to make sure

that his fellow villagers quickly surrounded him with an escort.

Tanabai made another rapid turn evading the pursuit. "Thank you, Gul'sary, thank you my beloved, my clever one," he whispered, as the horse, responding to the slightest pressure made off from their pursuers, twisting first one way and then the other.

The pacer completed the turn pressed to the ground and then straightened out. Now the men of the village had come up on either side and closed in behind; in a close-knit mass they made off at high speed. But again the pursuit nearly cut them off and they had to turn back and give ground. Like a flock of swift birds swinging in flight from one wing tip to the other the hordes of pursued and pursuers sped over the wide steppe. The air was full of dust, voices rang out, someone fell on top of his horse, another sailed over his horse's head and yet another was limping in pursuit of his horse. But all as one were seized with the delight and passion of the contest. In this game no one was responsible for himself. Daring and courage have the same mother . . .

The sun was already half below the horizon, it was getting dark but the *alaman-baiga* was still continuing in the blue chill of the evening, the ground still shaking with the pounding of hooves. The shouting had ceased, the pursuit over, but all were still riding on, intoxicated with the thrill of movement. They formed a great stretched-out line and rode from hillock to hillock caught in the power of the rhythm and music of their riding. Was it not because of this that faces grew intent and silent, and from this were born the murmuring sounds of the Kazakh *dombra* and the Kirgiz *komuz*?

Already they were coming up to the river. It was shining dimly ahead beyond the dark bushes. Only a little further over the river was the end of the contest where the village lay. Tanabai and those with him rode on as one. Gul'sary was in the middle like a flagship with its escorts.

But he was already tired, very tired. The day had been too hard and his strength was spent. Two riders, one on each side, held his bridle to stop him from falling. The others were covering his flanks and rear. Tanabai lay with his chest on top of the carcase, which was thrown across the saddle. His head was hanging and he could hardly keep in the saddle. If it was not for the help of the others neither he nor his mount would have been able to move. Thus, no doubt, long ago warriors raced away with their spoils and thus, no doubt, they would have saved a wounded chief from falling captive.

Now they came to the river, the meadow, and the wide pebbly ford just visible in the twilight.

The riders rode pell-mell into the water. It boiled and became cloudy. Through the clouds of spray and the deafening clatter of horseshoes they dragged the pacer across on to the far shore. It was over! Victory!

Someone took the carcase from Tanabai's saddle and rode ahead up to the village.

The Kazakhs stayed on the far bank.

"Many thanks for the games," the Kirgiz shouted.

"Good health to you! We'll meet you again in the autumn!" answered the others and turned their horses towards home.

It was already quite dark. Tanabai sat at table and the pacer stood tethered with the other horses in the yard. Gul'sary had never been so tired since his first day of breaking. But then he had been a youngster compared with what he was now. In the house they were talking about him.

"Let's drink, Tanabai, to Gul'sary's health; but for him we would not have seen victory today."

'Yes, the brown stallion was powerful as a lion. And that lad was strong, too. He'll go far over there."

"True. I can see now how Gul'sary escaped from their clutches; he just kept as close to the ground as the grass itself. The sight took my breath away."

"What more can one say? In the old days, the *batiry* would have ridden him on a foray. He's not a horse, but one of the *duldul* horses of legend."

"Tanabai, when are you going to put him to the mares?"

"He's already starting to show an interest in them, but it's too early yet. Next spring will be just right. In the autumn I'll let him graze and put a bit of flesh on . . ."

The men sat for a long time over the drinks, going over all the details of the *alaman-baiga* and the qualities of the pacer. Meanwhile he was in the yard drying off and chewing his bit. He would have to wait until dawn for his next feed. But it was not the hunger that was troubling him. His shoulders were aching, his legs hardly seemed to belong to him, his hooves were hot and the din of the *alaman-baiga* was resounding in his ears. He could still hear the shouts and the noise of pursuit. Now and again he shivered and snorted and pricked his ears. How he wanted to roll on the grass, stretch and wander with the other horses on the pasture. But his master was still inside, keeping him waiting.

Soon, however, out he came, swaying a little. There was some sort of sharp, burning smell coming from him. It was not often so. But a year would pass and the pacer would have to cope with a man who always reeked of this smell. He would hate that man and the abominable smell!

Tanabai came up to him, stroked his withers and put his hand under the cloth.

"Cooled off a bit? Tired? I'm as tired as the devil too. But don't look at me in that way—yes, I have been drinking, but we've been drinking your health. We've been celebrating. But only a little. I know how much I should take, you can be sure of that. I learnt about that at the war. Stop glancing at me like that, Gul'sary! Let's go out to the herd and get a rest . . ."

His master tightened the girth, exchanged a few words with the others who were now leaving the house; then all mounted and made off on their various ways.

Tanabai rode along the sleepy streets of the village. All was quiet. The windows were dark. There was the distant sound of a far-off tractor at work. The moon was high over the mountains; the apple trees were white with blossom in the gardens and a nightingale was singing. For some reason it was the only one near the village and was singing to itself alone; then it was silent, and then again started its liquid song.

Tanabai pulled up. "How beautiful it all is," he said, "and how quiet. Only the nightingale. Do you understand, Gul'sary? You want to go to the herd—yes, but I . . ."

They passed the smithy and from there had to go along the back street to the river and thence up to the herds. But his master somehow wished to go another way. He rode down the middle of the village and at the end he stopped by the house where that woman lived. Out ran the little dog who was always with the little girl, barked and then was quiet, wagging its tail. His master sat silent in the saddle, thought for a moment or two and then, with a sigh, unwillingly took up the reins.

The pacer went on. Tanabai turned down towards the river and once on the track urged the horse on. Gul'sary himself wanted to get to the herd as soon as possible. They crossed the meadow; up to the river the hooves rattled on the stones. The water was cold and noisy. But suddenly in the middle of the ford, his master pulled up with a sharp movement of the reins. Gul'sary shook his head, thinking that his master had made a mistake. They should not go back. How much further were they going? But, as if in answer, his master struck him on the flank. Gul'sary disliked it when the whip was used on him. He chewed the bit, displeased and then unwillingly obeyed and turned back. Once more across the meadow, once more along the track and once more back to that yard.

By the house his master began to fidget in the saddle, hesitating, moving the reins first one way and then the other. They had stopped by the gate. But, in fact, there were no gates; all that remained was one leaning post. Again the little dog ran out, barked and then was quiet, wagging its tail. All was silent and dark in the house.

Tanabai dismounted and walked in, leading the horse; he went up to the window and tapped on the glass.

"Who's there?" said a voice within.

"It's me, Byubyuzhan. Open up. It's me."

There was a little flash of light within the house and the window lit up dimly.

"What do you want? Why so late?"

Byubyuzhan had appeared at the door. She was in a white nightdress with open neck and with her dark hair falling over her shoulders. There was the warm smell of her flesh and the strange smell of that herb, unknown to Gul'sary.

"Forgive me," said Tanabai quietly. "I returned late from the *alaman*. I'm tired and the horse is quite worn out after the day. He should rest and you know yourself how far out the herds are now."

Byubyuzhan was silent.

Her eyes shone and then darkened, like the stones on the bottom of a pool lit by the moon. Gul'sary expected her to approach and stroke his neck, but she made no move.

"It's cold," Byubyuzhan shivered. "Well, what are you standing there for? Come in, if it's like that. You've got it all worked out." She laughed quietly. "I was quite exhausted myself with excitement when you were out there on the horse. Just like a child."

"I won't be a moment. I must tie up the horse."

"Put him in the corner over there by the windbreak."

Never had his master's hands shaken so much. He hurried taking off the bridle and had a lot of trouble with the girths; he only loosened one and forgot about the other entirely.

He went into the house together with her and the light in the window soon went out.

The pacer was not used to resting in a strange yard.

The moon was full. Looking over the windbreak, Gul'sary saw the mountains rising high above, lit up by the milky blue light of the night sky. His ears were all attention as he listened to the sounds of the night, the water gurgling in the ditch and far away the same tractor was still working and the same nightingale was singing in the gardens.

The white petals dropped quietly from the nearby apple tree on to the horse's head and mane.

It became lighter. The pacer stood there and shifted his weight from one leg to another, stood and patiently waited for his master. He was not to know that he would stand here many more times through a short night until the morning.

Tanabai left at dawn and saddled up Gul'sary with his warm hands which now carried the wild smell of that unknown herb.

Byubyuzhan came out to see him off. She clung to him and he gave her a long kiss.

"How your beard scratches," she whispered. "Hurry, look how light it's getting." She turned to go back into the house.

"Byubyu, come here," called Tanabai. "Do come back and stroke him, caress him." He nodded towards Gul'sary. "Don't insult us!"

"Oh, I forgot," she laughed. "Why, he's all covered in apple blossom," and murmuring gentle words she began to stroke

Gul'sary with her wonderful hands, soft and gentle like the lips of that little bay filly with the star on her forehead.

Once over the river his master began to sing. It was wonderful to move to his song and Gul'sary so wanted to get back as quickly as possible to the herd, to the pasture.

Tanabai was lucky during those May nights. Just then it was his turn for the night watch with the herd. And so there began a special sort of night life for the pacer. During the day he grazed and rested, and at night, after the herd had been rounded up into a hollow, his master sped on Gul'sary back to the same house again. And at dawn, while it was still dark, they raced back like horse thieves by little known steppe paths to the hollow where the horses had been left for the night. Here his master turned them out, counted them and at last began to calm down. It was hard on Gul'sary. His master went at top speed both ways, there and back, and it is none too easy to race at night over wild country. But that was what his master wanted to do.

Gul'sary would have liked something different. If the choice had been his he would not have left the herd. The power of a stallion was growing in him. So far he had got on with the herd stallion, but every day now they were more frequently clashing, chasing after the same filly. More and more often, arching his neck and lifting his tail high, Gul'sary would show off in front of the herd. He neighed, was excited and nipped the fillies' legs. They obviously appreciated this and followed him, rousing the envy of the stallion. The pacer had no easy time, for the stallion was an old and fierce fighter. However, it would have been far better to have been excited and to run away from the old stallion than to have to wait all night. How he missed the fillies! For a long time he stamped, striking the ground with his hooves and only quietened down later. Who knows how long these night journeys would have gone on, if something had not happened . . .?

On that night the pacer was standing in the yard as usual, longing to be with the herd, waiting for his master and was even dozing off. The reins were tied high up on a beam in the roof. He could not lie down and every time his head dropped, the bit pressed into the soft part of his mouth, but all the same he managed to sleep a little. There was a heaviness in the air and the sky was covered with thick dark clouds.

Suddenly through his dozing, as he was half asleep, Gul'sary heard the trees rustling and swaying as if something had come and begun to shake the trees to bring them down. The wind whipped around the yard, an empty bucket crashed and rattled and the washing flew off the line. The little dog whimpered and ran about not knowing where to go. Gul'sary angrily snorted and stood listening with pricked ears. Raising his head above the windbreak, he looked intently into the threatening darkness—out there, from the steppe, something terrible was approaching with a roar. In the very next moment the night broke up with a crashing noise like that of a felled tree falling, thunder rolled and the lightning cut the clouds apart. The rain came down in sheets. Gul'sary jerked at his halter as if he had been struck and, in despair, he neighed for his herd. There had awakened in him the ancient instinct to protect his kind from danger. The instinct told him to go to help them. In his madness he rampaged against his bit, the bridle, the hemp halter, against everything which held him so firmly to the spot. He began to panic, to dig at the ground with his hooves and neighed continuously in the hope of hearing the herd answer him. But there was only the whistling and howling of the storm. If only he could break loose!

His master rushed out in his shirt and after him the woman also in something white. They were soaked at once and darkened under the pouring rain. The blue sheet-lightning played over their wet faces and frightened eyes, picking out part of the house from the blackness and the door swaying in the wind.

"Whoa! Whoa!" yelled Tanabai at the horse as he tried to untie him. But the pacer did not recognise his master, he lunged at him, broke down the earth windbreak with his hooves and tore at the halter again and again. Tanabai succeeded in creeping up on him, by pressing against the wall and then, covering his head with his hands, bounded up and hung on the bridle.

"Unhitch him, quickly," he called to the woman. She had scarcely untied the rope when the rearing pacer was dragging Tanabai with him all over the yard.

"The *kamcha*!"

Byubyuzhan snatched up the whip and gave it to him.

"Whoa! whoa! I'll kill you," shouted Tanabai as he struck the horse about the head with the whip. He had to get into the saddle and out to the herd. What was happening out there? Where had the storm driven the horses?

But the pacer also had to get to the herd. This very minute the powerful force of his instinct was calling him to them in their hour of need. He neighed and pranced and made desperate efforts to break away. But the rain fell in an unbroken wall, the storm raged around, shaking with its thunder the night already torn up by the lightning.

"Hold him!" Tanabai gave the order and as Byubyuzhan seized the bridle he leapt into the saddle. He hardly touched it, hardly took up the reins before Gul'sary was off out of the yard, knocking over the woman into the puddles.

No longer heeding the bridle, whip or voice, Gul'sary raced through the stormy night, through the cutting rain, finding his way by scent alone. He carried his powerless master through the swollen river, through the cacophony of water and thunder, through bushes, through ditches, through ravines; unrestrained he hurtled on and on. Never before, not even in the great race nor at the *alaman-baiga*, had Gul'sary run as he did on that night of the hurricane.

Tanabai could not remember how or where his satanic pacer had carried him. The rain seemed to him to be a hot flame searing his face and body. "What's happening to the herd? Where are the horses now? Please God they have not run down to the railway. A terrible accident! Help me, Allah, help me! Help *arbaki*, my ancestors, where are you? Don't fall, Gul'sary, don't fall! Take us out to the steppe, out to the herd!"

Out on the steppe the white sheet-lightning played all the while, blinding the night with its white flame. Then once again the darkness closed in, the storm raged and the wind and rain came down.

Light, darkness, light and again darkness.

The pacer pranced and called with wide open mouth. He called and he called again, he searched, he waited. "Where are you? Where are you? Answer!" And in answer he heard only the thunder from the sky and then off he ran again, again he searched, again on into the storm . . .

Light, darkness, light and again darkness.

The storm died away only as morning came. The clouds dispersed gradually, but to the east the thunder went on rumbling, grumbling and dragging on. The tortured earth steamed. Several herdsmen rounded up the straggling horses.

But his wife was looking for Tanabai; more exactly, she did not search, but rather waited. During the night she had ridden out with the neighbours to help him. They found the herd and kept them in the shelter of a bank. But Tanabai was not with them. The others thought that he had got lost, but she knew he was not lost. When their neighbour's son shouted joyfully, "There he is, Dzhaidar-apa, here he comes!" and rode off to meet him, Dzhaidar did not move, she watched from her horse how her prodigal husband returned.

Silent and dreadful Tanabai rode up on his pacer who had gone lame during the night; his shirt was soaked and he had no hat. Gul'sary was limping on his off foreleg.

"We've been looking for you," announced the boy gaily, as he came up, "Dzhaidar-apa was already worried . . ."

Just like a boy!

"I got lost," muttered Tanabai.

Thus he met his wife. They said nothing to one another. When the boy rode off to drive the herd away from the precipice his wife said to him:

"Look at you, you didn't get dressed. Just as well that you've got your trousers and shoes on. Aren't you ashamed? You're no longer a young man. The children will soon have grown up, but you . . ."

Tanabai was silent. What could he say?

The boy meanwhile collected the herd together. All the horses and foals were safe.

"Let's go home, Altyke," called Dzhaidar to the boy. "We've all got lots to do. The *yurtas* have been scattered to the four winds. Let's go and see what we can salvage."

To Tanabai she said, "You stay here. I'll bring you something to eat and some more clothes. You can't appear like that in front of people."

"I'll be down there," said Tanabai.

They left. Tanabai drove the herd to their pasture a long way. The sun was now well out and it was warming up. The steppe

69

was steaming and had become alive again. There was a smell of rain and wet grass.

The horses slowly jogged on along the ridges and the stream beds and came out on the open plain. Here indeed another world opened out before Tanabai. The horizon was far, far away and marked with white clouds. The sky was wide, high, clear and on the horizon was the smoke from a train far out on the steppe.

Tanabai got down from his horse and walked over the grass. Up rose a lark climbing and singing. Tanabai walked with bowed head and suddenly fell to the ground.

Gul'sary had never seen his master like this. He lay face down and his shoulders shook with weeping. He was crying for shame and grief, he knew that he had lost that happiness which had been given to him for the last time in his life. And the lark still sang in the sky . . .

A day later the herd went up into the mountains. They would only return from there next year, in early spring. They wandered along the river, along the water meadows, past the village. The sheep flocks, the herds of goats and horses went past. The loaded camels and horses passed by with women and children in the saddles. Shaggy-coated dogs ran beside. The air was full of sounds, shouts, neighing and bleating.

Tanabai drove his herd across the big meadow, then along the hillock where not long before had been the noise of the crowd at the meeting; all the time he tried not to look towards the village. When Gul'sary suddenly started to pull over in that direction, towards the yard on the edge of the village, he was rewarded with a blow of the whip. So they did not go to see the woman with the wonderful hands, soft and gentle like the lips of that little bay filly with the star on her forehead . . .

The herd ran happily along.

How he wanted his master to sing, but he did not do so. The village, the *ail*, was far behind. Ahead are the mountains. Farewell, steppes, until next spring. Ahead are the mountains.

6

It was nearly midnight. Gul'sary could go no further. He had somehow struggled as far as the next ravine, stopping tens of times on the way, but he just could not get past the ravine. The old man, Tanabai, knew that he had no right to ask any more of the horse. Gul'sary groaned in agony, he groaned like a human. When he lay down, Tanabai did not stop him.

As he lay on the cold earth, the pacer continued to groan, his head rocking from side to side. He was cold and his whole body shivered. Tanabai flung off his coat and covered his horse with it.

'Feeling bad, are you? Very bad? You're frozen stiff, Gul'sary, and you've never been so chilled before."

Tanabai mumbled something else, but the pacer could no longer hear. His heart beats were now throbbing in his very head, they were deafening, breaking off now and again and faltering. Toom-tam-toom-tam, toom, toom, toom-tam, toom . . . as if the herd were running in panic from pursuers, who were hot on their heels.

The moon came out from behind the mountains, hanging in the mist over the earth. A shooting star fell and died . . .

"Lie here quietly. I'll go and get some brushwood," said the old man.

He wandered around for some time gathering up last year's dried weeds. His hands were scratched from the thorns as he gathered up an armful. He went further, down into the ravine, taking a knife with him in case of need and there he found some tamarisk bushes. He was glad, it would make a good fire.

Gul'sary had always feared a fire burning near him. But now he feared it no more, the warmth and smoke possessed him. Tanabai sat quietly on a sack throwing on bits of tamarisk together with the weeds and looked at the fire, warming his hands. Now and again he got up, adjusted the coat over the horse and sat down again by the fire.

Gul'sary had warmed up a bit, his shivering had stopped, but in his eyes there was a yellow mist, and a pain in his chest so that he could hardly breathe. The flames rose and fell with the wind. The old man was sitting before him, his old, old master and sometimes he disappeared and then appeared again. In his delirium it seemed to the pacer that they were riding again through the night of the storm, over the steppe; he was neighing and rearing, searching for the herd but could not find it. The white flashes of lightning burnt up and died away.

Light, darkness, light and darkness again . . .

7

Winter receded and finally went away for a time so that the shepherds realised that life is not always quite so hard. The warm days will come, the cattle will fatten up, there will be enough milk and meat, races and celebrations, busy days—lambing, shearing, rearing of the young animals, life in the nomadic camp. And in the midst of all of this each has his own personal life—love and parting, birth and death, pride in the success of children and dismay at bad news of their progress from boarding school; perhaps he would have studied more assiduously at home? Whatever else, there will always be enough worries and one can forget for a time about the trials of winter. Disease, murrain, glazed frost, leaking *yurtas,* and cold sheds will remain in the summaries and accounts until the next year. Then again winter will come back, galloping in on a white camel and will search out the shepherd, wherever he is, in the mountains or on the steppe and show him its tricks. He will remember everything that he had let slip from his mind for a time. Even in the twentieth century winter behaves just the same as ever . . .

It was all the same then. The scraggy flocks and herds came down from the mountains and spread out over the steppe. It was spring. They had lived through the winter.

That spring Gul'sary was a free stallion in the herd. Tanabai was sorry when now and again he had to saddle him, for it was indeed wrong to do so, as the season was upon them.

Gul'sary showed all the promise of being a good stallion. He looked after the foals like a father. A mare had only to glance up and he was there, stopping a foal from falling down somewhere or from leaving the herd. Gul'sary had another great virtue, he did not like the horses being alarmed; if that happened he immediately moved them quietly away.

That winter there had been changes at the *kolkhoz*. The new president had arrived. Choro had given up the post and was in the regional hospital. His heart had become very bad. Tanabai had every intention of visiting his old friend, but he could not get away. A herdsman, like a mother with a large family, is always busy, especially in the winter and in the spring. An animal is not like a machine which you can switch off and leave. So Tanabai was unable to get to the hospital. He had no assistant. His wife was listed as filling that post as she had to earn something. But although little was paid for the day's work, all the same one can get more for two persons' earning than for one.

But Dzhaidar had a young child. What sort of assistance could she give? She was busy day and night. Then, while Tanabai was trying to organise a relief, word came that Choro had left the hospital and had returned to the village. So they decided to visit him when they came down from the mountains. But they had only just got down to the valley and only just settled in, when something happened which Tanabai could never recall with equanimity . . .

The fame of a pacer has two sides to it. The more his fame spreads, the more the big-wigs covet him.

On that day Tanabai had driven the horses out to graze early and returned home for a meal. He sat there with his little daughter on his knee, drinking his tea and discussing family affairs with his wife.

He had to go and visit their son at his boarding school and at the same time go to the bazaar at the village and buy there some odds and ends of clothing for his wife and children at the old clothes shop.

"This time, Dzhaidar, I will saddle and ride the pacer," said Tanabai, "otherwise I will hardly have time to get there and back and get everything done. This will be the last time and then I'll let him be."

"As you think best," she agreed.

Outside there was the sound of approaching riders—someone had come to visit them.

"Take a look to see who it is," he said to his wife.

She went out and returned to say that it was the chief of the farm, Ibraim, and that there was someone else with him.

Tanabai got up unwillingly and went out of the *yurta*, still carrying his daughter. Although he disliked Ibraim, who was

74

zavkhoz, the man in charge of the horse breeding farm, it was the polite custom to go out to meet a guest. Tanabai did not himself know why he disliked Ibraim. Although he was pleasant, he gave no example to the others and there was something slippery or fishy about him. The main thing was that he himself did nothing, except render the accounts. There was no real direction to the horse breeding work, every herdsman was left to his own devices. Several times at party meetings Tanabai spoke about this; Ibraim agreed, thanked him for the criticism, but everything went on just as before. It was as well that honest herdsmen had been chosen—Choro had selected them himself.

Ibraim dismounted and came forward, his hands stretched out politely.

"Assalom aleikum, bai!" He called all the herdsmen "*bai*".

"Aleikum assalom!" answered Tanabai with reserve, as he pressed the other's hand.

"How are you? How are the horses, Tanabai, and you yourself?" Ibraim asked his usual questions and his fat cheeks made the usual smile.

"All is in order."

"Glory to God, I don't have to worry about you."

"Please come into the *yurta*."

Dzhaidar had spread out for the guests a new felt rug and on it a covering of goat skin, a special carpet for sitting on the floor.

Ibraim turned to her.

"Good morning, Dzhaidar-baibiche. Are you well? Are you looking after your *bai* well?"

"Good morning, please come and sit down."

Everyone sat down.

"Let us have some *kumys*," said Tanabai to his wife.

They drank the *kumys*, talking about this and that.

"This is the best job at this time—animal rearing. At least in summer you have milk and meat," pronounced Ibraim, "but out on the fields or other work, there's nothing. So isn't it best to be working with the herds or flocks, Dzhaidar-baibiche?"

Dzhaidar nodded and Tanabai was silent. He knew all this and had often heard such words from Ibraim, who never let slip a chance to remark that one should appreciate work with the animals. Tanabai wanted to say that it was not much good if people hold on to their comfortable jobs because there is milk and meat. What about the others? How long will people work for nothing extra? Was it like this before the war? Each autumn two or three cart loads of grain were brought to each house. And now? They run around with empty sacks, trying to get something some-where. They grow grain but have none for themselves. What good is this? You won't get far on meetings or exhortations alone. It had broken Choro's heart that, except for fine words, he could give nothing to people for their work. But it was useless to talk about this painful business to Ibraim. Indeed Tanabai did not wish to prolong this polite conversation now. He had to send them on their way quickly, saddle the pacer and get off to do his jobs and get back again. Why were they visiting him? He couldn't very well ask outright.

"I don't think that I know you, brother?" Tanabai addressed Ibraim's companion, a young and silent *dzhigit*. "Was Abalak your father, by any chance?"

"Yes, Tanake, I am his son."

"Ah, how time flies. Have you come to look at the herds? Are you interested in them?"

"Oh, no, we . . ."

"He has come with me," Ibraim interrupted. "We're here about some little business; we'll talk about that later. Dzhaidar-baibiche, your *kumys* is simply wonderful, it has a strong aroma. Do pour me another cup."

Again they talked about this and that, Tanabai felt that there was something unpleasant in the air, but he could not think what it could be to have brought Ibraim to visit him. At last Ibraim took a piece of paper from his pocket.

"Tanake, we have come to see you about this matter—read this paper."

Tanabai read it to himself, word by word, and as he read he just could not believe his eyes. Written in blurred letters on the paper was:

"Order. To Herdsman Bakasov,
    Send the pacer, Gul'sary, to the stables for riding pur-poses.

                        President of the Kolkhoz."

Underneath was an indecipherable signature and the date, 5th March, 1950.

Flabbergasted by such an unexpected turn of events, Tanabai silently folded the paper into four and put it in the breast pocket of his tunic and sat for a long time, looking at the ground. He felt cold in the pit of his stomach. Of course, this was not really unusual. He bred the horses in order to give them to others for work or riding. How many he had already sent to the brigades over the years. But give up Gul'sary? This was more than he could stand. Feverishly he considered how to hold on to the pacer. He would have to think carefully and keep himself under control. Ibraim was beginning to look worried.

"It was on account of this little matter that we called in on you, Tanake," he explained cautiously.

"Well, Ibraim," Tanabai looked calmly at him, "this matter will not run away. Let us have some more *kumys* and talk it over."

"Well, certainly, of course, you are a sensible fellow, Tanake."

"Sensible! Go to two devils with your fancy words!" Tanabai kept his angry thoughts to himself.

Once again they talked meaningless platitudes. Now there was no need to hurry.

This was Tanabai's first encounter with the new president—or more exactly with his illegible signature. He had not yet seen him. He had been wintering up in the mountains when the new man had come to replace Choro. They said that he was a stern man and had been an important official. At the very first meeting he had warned that he would punish the negligent severely and he threatened with the courts those who failed to work the minimum amount of working days. He said that all the difficulties in the *kolkhoz* system were because the collectives were too small, now they would form bigger units and soon matters would improve; that was why he had been sent here and his main task would be to carry on the work in accordance with all the rules of agro- and zootechnics. To this end all would have to study in classes on these subjects.

Indeed this training had been put in hand—placards had been put up and lectures started. But if the shepherds fell asleep during the lectures, that was their affair.

"Tanake, we must be getting along," Ibraim looked at Tanabai in anticipation and started to draw up his boot tops and shake out and smooth his foxskin cap.

"Well, *zavkhoz*, tell the president that I will not hand over Gul'sary. He is my herd stallion. He is serving the mares."

"Oho. Tanake, we can give you five stallions in his place. No mare will be left unserved. Is that your only trouble?"

Ibraim was amazed. He had been sure that everything had been going well and then, suddenly ... If it had not been Tanabai, but someone else, the matter would have been quickly dealt with. But Tanabai was Tanabai; he had not even spared his own brother and one must take account of his character. One must tread carefully.

"I don't need your five stallions." Tanabai wiped his wet brow, was silent for a moment and then decided to come straight to the point.

"This man, your president, hasn't he anything to ride? Have all the horses at the stable been sent away? Why is Gul'sary especially necessary?"

"How can you talk like that, Tanake. The president is our chief, he deserves respect. He goes to the regional centre and people come to him. He must look like a president in the eyes of the people, one might say."

"One might say what? Would no one recognise him on another horse? And if he is to be on show, why must it be on the pacer?"

"It's not necessarily 'must', but it certainly should be so. You, Tanake, were a soldier during the war. Did you go around in a staff car and the general in a truck? No, the general had the staff car and you rode in a truck. That's reasonable, isn't it?"

"That's quite another matter," said Tanabai, not too sure of himself. He did not and could not explain why it was another matter. Then, feeling that the ring was closing around the pacer, he said angrily, "I won't give up the pacer. If I'm no good, then take me off the work with the herd and I'll go back to the smithy. There at least you won't want to take away my hammer."

"Why are you taking it this way, Tanake? We respect you and value your work. But you're behaving like a boy. Is it worthy of you?"

Ibraim began to fidget. He had got into a fine mess. He had promised, suggested the idea, volunteered to go about it and now this obstinate type was wrecking the whole thing.

Ibraim sighed deeply and turned to Dzhaidar.

"What do you think, Dzhaidar-baibiche; what is one horse or pacer, more or less? In the herd there are all sorts of horses, choose any of them. They have sent me and I have come . . ."

"What are you so concerned about, then?" asked Dzhaidar.

Ibraim hesitated, waved his hands.

"What? Discipline. I was given the order, I'm a small person. It's not for me. I could ride on a donkey. You can ask him, the son of Abalak, he was sent to collect the pacer."

The horseman nodded silently.

"It's not very good," continued Ibraim. "They sent us the president, he is our guest and we cannot, from the whole village, give him a decent horse. People will find out. What will they say? Has anything like this happened with the Kirgiz before?"

"That's all right," remarked Tanabai, "let the village know. I will go and see Choro. Let him consider the matter."

"Do you think that Choro will advise you not to hand over the horse? He was consulted. You won't do him any good, it would be a sort of sabotage. As if we did not recognise the new president's authority, but go and complain to the former one. Also Choro is ill; why spoil his relationship with the president? He will have to work closely with the new president in his new job as *partorg* (party work organiser). Why mess things up . . .?"

Now they were talking about Choro, Tanabai was silent. No one said a word.

Dzhaidar sighed deeply.

"Give him to them," she said to her husband, "don't keep them waiting."

"That's the right thing to do and should have been decided long ago. Thank you, Dzhaidar-baibiche."

Ibraim was right to be grateful. Not long afterwards he was promoted to the post of the *kolkhoz* president's deputy on live-stock matters from his post in charge of the horse breeding.

Tanabai sat in the saddle, his eyes cast down, but he missed nothing. He saw how they caught Gul'sary and a new halter was put on—Tanabai would not give them his for anything. He could see that Gul'sary did not wish to leave the herd but strained at the halter held by Abalak's son as Ibraim beat him with full force, riding up first on one side, then on the other. He saw the eyes of the pacer, the troubled look of the horse who could not understand why he was being taken from his mares and foals and from his master. He saw how the breath came from his wide-open mouth as he neighed, saw his mane, back, croup, the marks of the whip on his flanks; he could see all the markings, even the little patch of chestnut on his right foreleg above the fetlock, saw his step, the marks of his hooves on the ground; he saw every-thing, even the smallest hair of his light yellow dun coat—he saw everything and bit his lip, suffering in silence. When he raised his head, those who had taken away Gul'sary were already out of sight behind the hill. Tanabai shouted and spurred his horse after them.

"Stop, don't you dare." Dzhaidar ran out from the *yurta*.

As he rode off he was suddenly seized with the awful sus-picion—his wife was having her revenge on the pacer for those nights. He turned his horse round sharply and, beating him with the whip, rode back. He stopped near the *yurta,* jumped down and ran with a terrible expression on his face to his wife.

"Why did you? Why did you say 'Give him to them'?" he whispered looking directly at her.

"Be reasonable; put your hands down." Quietly and calmly as ever, she restrained him. "Listen to what I have to say. Is Gul'sary your horse? Your very own? What have you got of your own? Everything we have belongs to the *kolkhoz*. This is how we live. The pacer also belongs to the *kolkhoz*. The president is in charge of the *kolkhoz*; what he says goes. You need not think that the other matter comes into this. You can leave at once! Go on! Leave me! She is better than me, more beautiful, younger. She's a fine woman. I could have been a widow too, but you came back. How long did I have to wait for you? But don't let's take that into account. You have three children. What's to become of them? What will you say to them? What will they say? What shall I say to them? Make up your own mind . . ."

Tanabai went out on the steppe. He was alone with the herd until dusk; he just could not calm down. The herd was or-phaned. His soul was orphaned too. The pacer had carried that away with him. Everything had gone away with him. Nothing was the same. The sun was not the same, nor the sky, and he himself was changed.

He returned when it was dark. He walked into the *yurta* silent, looking black with anger. The girls were already asleep. The fire burnt brightly. His wife poured water on his hands and gave him his supper.

"No, thank you," Tanabai refused. Then he said:

"Take the *temir-komuz*, play me the Camel's Lament."

Dzhaidar picked up the *temir-komuz* and put it to her lips, touched the steel cord with her finger, breathed on it and then breathed in, making the ancient music of the nomads. The song is about the she-camel who has lost her little white camel. She runs for many days over the desert. She seeks and calls her young one. She grieves that she no longer leads him above the ravine in the morning or the evening; that no longer can they pluck the leaves from the branch or walk over the rippling sands nor wander over the meadows in spring, nor can she feed him with her white milk. Where are you, my little dark-eyed camel? Answer me? The milk is flowing from my teats, from the full udder. White milk ...

Dzhaidar played the *temir-komuz* well. Long ago he had fallen in love with her because of that, when she was still a young girl.

Tanabai listened, his head bowed and once again saw everything without looking. Her hands, roughened by many years of work in heat and cold; her greying hair, the wrinkles on her neck, by her mouth and by her eyes.

Her vanishing youth had gone with the coming of those wrinkles—the small dark girl with the shoulder-long hair had gone, as had his youth and their former closeness. He knew that she was not noticing him. She was absorbed in her music and in her thoughts. He saw there a half of his own troubles and suffering for she had always shared them.

... the camel runs for many days; she seeks and calls her young one. Where are you, little dark-eyed camel? The milk is flowing from my teats, from the full udder and down the legs. Where are you? Answer me? The milk is flowing from my teats, from my full udder. White milk ...

The girls slept on in one another's arms. Outside the *yurta* lay the steppe—vast and impenetrable in the dark of the night.

At that time Gul'sary was rampaging in the stable; he did not let the stable lads sleep. It was the first time he had been in such a stable, a prison for horses.

8

It was a great joy for Tanabai when one morning he saw that the pacer was out with the herd; he had a broken halter hanging from his bridle and he was saddled up.

"Gul'sary! Good morning, Gul'sary!" Tanabai rode up quickly and saw him close to with his strange bridle and with a strange unwieldy saddle with heavy stirrup leathers. But what really upset him was the smart velvet cushion on the saddle, as if not a man but a fat-arsed old woman rode him. Tanabai spat with disgust. He wanted to catch the horse and throw off all this nonsensical tack, but Gul'sary evaded him and made off. The pacer had no time for him, he wanted to be off after the mares. He missed them so much that he did not even notice his former master.

"So you've escaped, broken the halter. Stout fellow, go and enjoy yourself, enjoy your freedom, I won't tell on you," thought Tanabai and decided to let the herd run. Let Gul'sary feel quite at home again—until they catch up with him.

"Kai-kait-kait," called Tanabai, standing up in his stirrups and waving his *ukruk*, he drove the herd out.

The mares moved off, calling the foals, the young fillies ran out prancing. The wind was in their manes. The new green earth was laughing in the sunshine. Gul'sary shook himself, straightened up and strutted before them. He took up his position at the head of the herd, drove off the stallion who had taken his place, pushed him down on to his haunches and showed off in front of the herd. He neighed and danced and ran off first one way and then the other. The scent of the herd was intoxicating—the smell of the mare's milk, the smell of the foals and the spicy smell of the wind. He did not care that he was still carrying that ridiculous saddle with the ridiculous velvet cushion on it or that the heavy stirrup leathers were beating against his flanks. He forgot that yesterday he had been standing in the town at the big tethering rail and had chewed at his bit and started at the noisy lorries. He had forgotten that later on he had stood in a puddle by that filthy pub and his new master had come out with his friends, all reeking of vodka, and then his new master had belched and wheezed on his back. He had forgotten how on the way home they had raced, like the fools they were, through the mud. He had carried his master at full career and his master had slumped in the saddle like a sack and then had snatched at the reins and beaten him about the head with the whip.

The pacer had forgotten it all, for the scent of the herd was intoxicating—the smell of the mares' milk, the smell of the foals, the spicy smell of the wind. The pacer ran on and on, not suspecting that his pursuers were catching up with him.

Tanabai brought the herd back to the original grazing place; two horsemen hurried down from the village. Again they led Gul'sary away from the herd and back to the stable.

But he soon appeared again; this time without bridle or saddle. Somehow he had succeeded in throwing off the halter and had escaped by night from the stable. At first Tanabai laughed, then he was silent and having thought things over he caught the pacer with the *ukruk*. He brought him in himself, put on a halter and led him to the village where he persuaded a young herdsman from near-by to help him by riding behind the pacer to push him on. Half-way to the town they met the stable hands coming after the runaway. Handing over Gul'sary to them, Tanabai shouted at them,

"What sort of hopeless people are you, that you cannot look after the president's horse? Tie him up better next time!"

When Gul'sary came the third time, Tanabai was really angry. "You are a fool! What devil brings you here? You really are a fool." He swore at the pacer as he chased after him with the *ukruk*. He took him back again and again had a slanging match with the stable hands.

But Gul'sary did not want to learn sense; he ran away whenever he could. He made the stable hands and Tanabai fed up.

But one day Tanabai slept late for he had come back very late from the pasture the night before. He had brought the herd close to the *yurta* in case of trouble and fallen asleep. But it was an uneasy sleep. He had had a long and tiring day. He dreamed a

84

strange and terrible dream. He was at the war again or at some other fight. There was blood everywhere and his hands were covered with it. Even as he slept, he thought to himself that no good would come of this dream of blood. He wanted to wash his hands, but everyone was shoving him, mocking him with raucous laughter . . . and someone, he did not know who, was shrieking at him, "Tanabai, you're washing your hands in blood, in blood. There's no water, Tanabai, everywhere blood! Ha-ha, ho-ho, hee-hee!"

"Tanabai, Tanabai, wake up!" His wife was shaking him.

"What is it? What is it?"

"Can't you hear, something is going on outside, with the herd! The stallions are fighting. No doubt Gul'sary has run away again and is here."

"Damn and blast him! I've no peace at all." Tanabai dressed quickly, seized his *ukruk* and ran out to the hollow, where a struggle was going on. It was already quite light.

He ran and then saw Gul'sary. But what on earth was this? The pacer was prancing, held by double hobbles, iron fetters, the fetters were clanging; he was shying, groaning, neighing. And this lop-eared herd stallion was kicking and biting at him, as he liked.

"You monster!" Tanabai flew at him and dragged away the lop-eared one so that the *ukruk* broke. He drove him off. Tears filled Tanabai's eyes, "What have they done to you, eh? Who had the idea of fettering you? And why did you have to drag yourself here, you wretched dolt?"

But he had had to . . . such a long way it had been, over the river, through the ditches and over the hillocks, hopping here in the fetters to reach his herd. No doubt it had taken all night, hopping and walking along. Alone, rattling his chains like a runaway prisoner.

"Well, well." Tanabai shook his head. He stroked the pacer and put his face by the horse's lips. Gul'sary snuffled at him with his lips, tickled him and screwed up his eyes.

"What are we going to do? Give this up, Gul'sary. It won't do you any good in the end. You're a silly, foolish old chap. You don't know what you're doing."

Tanabai inspected the pacer. The bites and scratches from the

85

stallion's attack would heal. But his legs had been severely rubbed by the fetters. His pasterns and hooves were bleeding. The felt covering of the fetters was rotten and moth-eaten. When the horse had jumped into the river water, the covering had come off, exposing the iron of the fetters. It was this which had cut his legs.

"Only Ibraim would have dug out such fetters from one of the old men. This is his work," thought Tanabai angrily. "Yes, and indeed there's more to it than that." The *kishen*, the fetters, were of the old chain type. Each had its special lock and it was impossible to open it without the proper key. In the old days they put them on the best horses so that the horse stealers could not drive them away from the pasture. Ordinary hobbles of rope could be cut with a knife and that was that. But with chain fetters, you couldn't get the horse away. But that was long, long ago and now this sort of fetter was a rarity. Some old fellow had probably kept these as a relic of the past. When it was needed someone had told Ibraim. They had fettered the pacer, so that he could not go far from the village pasture. But he had got away all the same . . .

The whole family joined in the task of taking the fetters from Gul'sary's legs. Dzhaidar held the bridle and covered his eyes, the two daughters played near-by, while Tanabai, sweating profusely, brought up all the resources of his toolkit and tried to pick the lock. All his skill from the smithy days was needed; he puffed away, hurt his hands, but eventually found a way to open the lock.

He flung the fetters out of sight, put ointment on the pacer's wounded legs and Dzhaidar led him away to tether him. The elder daughter lifted up the younger and they all went into their home.

Tanabai sat there, out of breath, exhausted after the effort. Then he collected his tools together and went to pick up the fetters; he had to return them, otherwise he would have to answer for that, too. He looked at the rusted objects and was amazed at the workmanship. All was beautifully made, well thought out for the purpose. It was the work of old Kirgiz smiths. Yes, their craft was gone, forgotten for ever. No longer are such fetters needed. Other things have disappeared, too, and what a pity! They knew in the old days how to make such decor-

86

ated things, of silver, copper and wood, and of leather. The old things were not necessarily costly, but they were beautiful. Each on its own was unique. Now they are no longer made. Now everything is made of aluminium—mugs, cups, spoons, earrings and plates, whatever you want, it's all the same. Dull. The last of the old saddlers are just surviving. What saddles they used to make! Each saddle had its own history, who and for whom he had made it, and how he was rewarded for his work. Soon everyone will go around in cars, as in Europe. Everyone in similar machines, which you can only tell apart by their numbers. But we forget about the skills of our grandparents. The old handicrafts have been buried for ever; are not the soul and eyes of a man in his handiwork?

Tanabai was given to such trains of thought; he would go on with his views about the local people's craft and was annoyed about it and did not know whom to blame for its disappearance. But in his youth he himself had been one of the gravediggers for old things. Once, even, he had made a speech at a *komsomol* meeting called for the liquidation of the *yurta*. He had heard someone say that the *yurta* should go, that it was a pre-revolutionary dwelling.

"Down with the *yurta*! We've lived long enough in the old way."

And so they had treated the *yurta*, as they had the *kulaks*. They had begun to build houses and the *yurtas* had been scrapped. The sheeting had been cut up for various purposes, the wood parts made into fences or hurdles and even cut up for firewood.

It had turned out afterwards that nomadic animal husbandry was quite impracticable without the *yurta*. Every time that he thought about it now Tanabai was amazed that he had been able to speak as he had, to swear at the *yurta*. So far no one had been able to think of anything better. How had he failed to see in the *yurta* a remarkable invention of his people in which every small detail had been proved by the experience of generations over the long centuries?

Now he was living in a leaking, soot-impregnated *yurta*, left to him by the old man, Torgoi. It was very many years old and it had only held together due to the long-suffering Dzhaidar. She

87

was busy mending it for days on end; she patched it up to make it habitable and in a week or two she was having to repair it again; the roof had given way, again there was a gaping hole, through which the wind blew, the snow or the rain leaked. She got to work once more and mended it, but there was no sign of an end to this sequence.

"How long will we suffer like this?" she would complain "This is not a sheet for the roof, but rubbish; it falls apart like sand, and the supports, what a state they are in. It's shameful. At least you should see that they give us a new roof sheeting. Are you head of the family or not? We should at least live like human beings."

At first Tanabai used to calm her down and promised to do something. But when he was next in the village and he remembered that he had to ask about a new *yurta,* it turned out that the old makers of *yurtas* had died long ago and none of the young men had any idea of how to make them. Further there was no sheeting for a *yurta* in the *kolkhoz.*

"All right, give me some wool. We'll make up our own covering," proposed Tanabai.

"What wool?" they answered. "Have you just come down from the moon? All the wool has to be sold to meet the plan and we are not supposed to keep a gram even for our own use." They offered a tent instead.

Dzhaidar sharply refused this. "Better to live in a leaking *yurta,* than in a tent."

At that time many of the herdsmen had had to start living in tents. But what sort of a dwelling was it? You couldn't stand up in it, sit down or light a fire. In summer it was unbearably hot, and in winter you couldn't keep a dog in there it was so cold.

"You can't put your things out, fix up a kitchen or make things nice and comfortable. When some visitors call, you have no idea where to put them.

"No, no," went on Dzhaidar, "do what you like, but I cannot live in a tent. It may be all right for those without a family—and only then for a short time—but we have a family. We have children. We have to bath them and bring them up; no, I won't have anything to do with the idea."

Tanabai met Choro then and told him all about it.

"How has this happened, president?"

88

Choro sadly shook his head.

"You and I should have thought about this earlier, and our superiors, too. We can write letters about it now, but we don't know what they'll have to say. They say that wool is a valuable raw material. Deficit. Export. To use it in the home economy for household use is, they say, inexpedient."

Tanabai was silent after this. It seemed that he was partly responsible and he mocked himself for his past stupidity, "Inexpedient. Ha-ha! Inexpedient."

For a long time this cruel word would not leave his head, "inexpedient".

So they lived on in their old patched up and patched up again *yurta*, whose roof covering needed only ordinary wool to mend it. Incidentally they sheared this wool by the ton from the flocks of their own *kolkhoz* ...

Tanabai went into his *yurta* with the fetters in his hands. The *yurta* seemed so squalid that he was filled with rage against himself, against the fetters which had so slashed the pacer's legs, and his teeth ground together. Just then, on top of everything else, up galloped the stable hands, hurrying after Gul'sary.

"Take him back," shouted Tanabai at them and his lips quivered with rage. "And give these fetters to the president and tell him from me that if he once again puts them on the pacer, I'll brain him with them. Go and tell him that."

It was foolish to have said that. Alas, how foolish. His fervour and straight-speaking was never to cost him so dear ...

9

It was a bright sunny day. Spring was blinking at the sun, curling the new young leaves, steaming in the furrows and breaking out in the grass underfoot.

Near the stable some boys were playing tip-cat. Some smart boy would throw the "cat" in the air and strike it with force along the road. Then they measured the distance with a stick; one, two, three, seven, ten, fifteen ... The carping judges went along in a throng, checking carefully that the measurer made no mistake. Twenty-two.

"It was seventy-eight and now twenty-two," the boy counted and totalled, then cried out with delight, "It's a hundred, a hundred!"

"Hurrah, a hundred!" Others took up the cry.

There it was. They'd made it exactly, without falling short or going over.

Now the loser had to do the "piping". The victor went to the point of throwing and again hit the "cat" as far as he could. Everyone ran to the point where it had fallen and then from there he had to strike again, in all three times. The loser was almost crying because he would have to "pipe" so far. But the rules of the game are firm. "What are you standing there for, get piping!"

The piper breathes in deeply, filling his lungs and runs chanting,

> 'Akbai, Kokbai,
> Don't chase the calves in the meadow,
> If you do, you won't catch them,
> You'll just get scolded, dooo, ooooo ... "

His head is already splitting, but he still pipes on. No, he hasn't reached the starting point. He must go back and start again. Once again he doesn't make it. The victor is delighted. "If you haven't enough wind, then let me ride you." He climbs up on to the piper's back and the latter carries him, as if he were a donkey.

"Off you go, faster, faster." The rider kicks with his feet. "Look, fellows, this is my Gul'sary. Watch how he paces."

But Gul'sary himself was standing behind the stable wall and he was bored. They hadn't saddled him today. Neither had they fed or watered him since morning. They had forgotten. The stable was empty, except for him in his stall, the carts had all gone out and the riding horses were all out . . .

The stable hands were mucking out. The boys were still playing noisily over the wall. How he would love to go to the herd, out to the steppe. He could see in imagination the open valley, how the herds wandered and grazed. Above them flew the grey geese, their wings flapping, and calling to one another . . .

Gul'sary snatched, trying to break the halter. No, they had fastened him firmly to the chains. Perhaps his herd could hear him? Gul'sary stretched his head towards the window under the roof and, stamping his hooves, neighed a long and resonant call, "Where are you?"

"Be quiet, you devil!" A stable boy jumped in and waved a spade threateningly at him; he then turned and called out through the door, "Shall we bring him out?"

"Bring him out," a voice answered.

Now two stable lads led him out. How bright it was and what lovely air. The thin nostrils of the pacer quivered, touching and drawing in the intoxicating spring air. There was a bitter smell of leaves and one of wet mud. The blood was coursing through him. If only he could run. Gul'sary pranced a bit.

"Whoa, whoa there." At once several voices shouted at him.

Why were there so many people around him today? They had rolled-up sleeves, healthy, hairy arms. One in a grey overall was laying out some shiny metal objects on a white cloth. They shone so much in the sun that it hurt his eyes. Others had ropes. Oh, and his new master is here, too; looking very important with his short fat legs apart in their wide breeches. His brows are knitted like those of everyone else, only his sleeves are not rolled up. He had one hand on his hip, with the other he was fiddling with a button on his tunic. Yesterday he had been reeking again with that awful smell.

91

"What are we waiting for, let's start? Shall we begin, Dzhoro-kul Aldanovich?" Ibraim turned to the president, who nodded silently.

"Off we go, then," said Ibraim and hurriedly hung his foxskin cap on a nail by the door. It fell off, straight into the muck. Ibraim delicately picked it up, shook it and hung it up again.

'You'd better go a little further away, Dzhorokul Aldanovich, or perhaps you'll be unlucky and get kicked. Horses are dumb animals, you can always expect a dirty trick from them."

Gul'sary shivered as a lasso came over his head. It was prickly. It was then tied with a running noose to his chest and the end was put out at one side. What was this for? Then they put another lasso on his hind leg, on the ankle and again were hob-bling his legs. Gul'sary began to be worried, snorted and his eyes glanced from side to side. What was all this about?

"Quickly," Ibraim was in a hurry and spoke in an unex-pectedly high voice. "Get on with it."

Two pairs of strong hairy arms took up the rope with a sharp pull. Gul'sary fell to the ground as if struck down. Ugh. The sun twisted over and the earth shook from his weight. What is all this? Why was he lying on his side, why were the people's faces so long and drawn out and the trees up there? Why was it so uncomfortable to lie on the ground? No, this would not do.

Gul'sary shook his head and strained with all his strength. The lassos cut in and dragged his legs up to his belly. The pacer tried to break loose again, to strain, desperately he twisted his free hind leg. The lasso tightened and creaked.

"Now hold him down with the knees and press him down," said Ibraim.

Everyone ran up and pressed him down with their knees.

"Hold his head to the ground. Tie him. Tighter there. That's right. Quicker. A bit tighter there, once more, a bit more. That's all right, now tie these with a knot." Ibraim gave a continuous string of orders.

The legs of the pacer were shackled even tighter with the nooses until they were held in one cruel knot. Gul'sary groaned and grunted, trying to free himself from the deadly nooses and to throw off the men who were sitting on his head and neck. But they again applied pressure with their knees. A convulsion swept through the pacer's wet body, his legs went cold and he gave in.

"Phew! At last!"

"He's a strong one."

"Now he won't move, not even if he were a tractor!"

Now his new master, that man, ran up to the horse and squatted on his haunches by the head, pouring out the smell of yesterday's stale drink and smiled with open hate and triumph, as if there lay before him not his horse, but his most loathed enemy.

By him squatted Ibraim, wiping his face with his handkerchief. They squatted there together smoking, awaiting the next part of the act.

Outside the boys played on at their tip-cat.

> "Akbai, Kokbai,
>   Don't chase the calves in the meadow,
>   If you do, you won't catch them,
>   You'll just get scolded, dooo, ooooo . . ."

The sun was still shining and for the last time he saw in his imagination the great steppe, saw how the herds wandered there at liberty. Above them flew the grey geese with flapping wings and calling one to another. But his mouth was covered with flies and he could not drive them off.

"Shall we begin, Dzhorokul Aldanovich?" Ibraim asked again. The other nodded, again silently and Ibraim got up.

Everyone moved to apply full pressure again with knees and chests on the captive horse. They pressed his head more firmly to the ground. Some hands were at work between his hind legs.

The boys climbed up on to the fence, like a flock of sparrows.

"Look, fellows, what are they doing?"

"They are cleaning his hooves."

"Fat lot you know. Hooves, indeed."

"Oi, what do you want, go away," Ibraim waved them away. "Go and play, this is nothing to do with you."

The boys got down quickly from the fence.

It was quiet.

Gul'sary stiffened from the blows and pressure and the touch of something cold. His new master squatted there in front of him, watching, waiting for something. Suddenly there was a dreadful pain which exploded like a flash in his eyes. Oh! There seemed to be a bright red flash and then everything went black, quite black ...

When all was over Gul'sary lay there a long time, still tethered. The blood had to clot.

"Well, that's done, Dzhorokul Aldanovich, now everything will be all right," said Ibraim, wiping his brow. "Now he will never run away again. His running away days are over now. Don't pay any heed to Tanabai. Spit on him. He was always like that. He didn't pity his own brother; he had him sent off as a *kulak* to Siberia. He wouldn't wish well to anyone ..."

The satisfied Ibraim took his foxskin cap from the nail; shook it, smoothed it down and put it on his sweaty head.

The boys played on at their tip-cat,

> "Akbai, Kokbai,
> Don't chase the calves in the meadow,
> If you do, you won't catch them,
> You'll just get scolded, dooo, ooooo ..."

"Aha, you couldn't make it, bend down. Off you go, Gul'sary, off you go. Hurrah, look at my Gul'sary!"

It was a bright, sunny day ...

IO

It was night. The depth of night. Old man and old horse. The fire burnt on the edge of the ravine. The flame rose and fell in the wind . . .

The hard frozen earth was chilling the pacer's side. His chest felt heavy; his head was tired and moved up and down as it had under the weight of the fetters.

But, as then, Gul'sary could not run or break what was hampering him. He wanted to move his legs freely, so that his hooves became hot from running, he wanted to fly over the ground, to breathe deeply, to race as fast as possible to the pasture, to neigh with full voice, calling together his herd, so that the mares and foals ran with him over the great steppe. But the fetters would not let him. Alone with the ringing sound of the chain, like a runaway prisoner he walked, hopping step after step. All was empty, dark and lonely. The moon was shining up in the wind; it rose before his eyes as he raised his head and fell, like a stone, when he let his head drop.

Now light, now darkness, now light, and darkness again. His eyes were too tired to look.

The chains rattled, rubbing his legs until the blood came. One hop, then another, one more. Dark, emptiness. How far it was to walk in the fetters, how hard to walk.

The fire burnt on the edge of the ravine. The hard frozen earth was chilling the pacer's side . . .

I I

Two weeks later they had to go off again for the grazing, once more into the mountains with the herds. For the whole summer, all the autumn and the winter until the next spring. It's bad enough to move from one place to another. Where does all this stuff come from? Because of this there is an ancient Kirgiz saying, "If you think you are poor, try the life of a nomad."

They had to spend a night in the town in order to get through all the necessary preparations—visit the mill, the bazaar, the shoe-maker, to see their son at his boarding school. Tanabai went round like someone who had fallen into the water. He seemed very strange to his wife. At dawn he was in a hurry, couldn't say a word and went straight off out to the herd. Then he came back to dinner, stonily silent and annoyed. It was as if he was on the alert, expecting something to happen . . .

"What's wrong with you?" asked Dzhaidar.

He did not answer at once, but then said, "I had a bad dream not so long ago."

"Is that a reason to leave me alone and not talk?"

"No, truly. It just will not get out of my head."

"Well, what times we live in. Weren't you the founder of the atheists in the village? Wasn't it on you that the old women heaped their curses? You're getting old, Tanabai, you spend all your time out with the heard. But now you've got this summer grazing to get ready for and you're not worried about it as you should be. How do you think I will get on with the children? At least you might go and see Choro. Decent people call to see their sick friends before going out with the herds."

"I'll get around to it, later."

"What do you mean later? Are you afraid of going to the village. Let's all go together tomorrow. We'll take the children. I've got some things to do there, too."

Next day having arranged with a young neighbour to keep an

eye on the herd, they all rode off on horseback. Dzhaidar took the younger daughter and Tanabai the elder. They carried the children in front of them on the saddle.

They rode through the village street, greeting friends whom they met and, near the smithy, Tanabai suddenly stopped.

"Wait a minute," he said to his wife. He got down and lifted his elder daughter up behind his wife on the horse's croup.

"What are you going to do? Where are you off to?"

"I'll be back in a moment, Dzhaidar, you ride on and tell Choro that I'll be looking in shortly. I've got some important business to deal with in the office and it will soon be shutting for dinner. I must also call at the smithy. I need some spare shoes and other gear for the journey."

"I don't like going on alone."

"Don't worry, I'll catch you up in a minute or two. You go on."

Tanabai called neither at the office nor at the smithy. He went straight to the stables.

Meeting no one he went into the stable. While his eyes were getting accustomed to the darkness, his mouth became dry. It was quiet and empty in the stable, all the horses were out. Looking round, Tanabai sighed with relief. So he went out of a side door into the yard to have a word with one of the stable boys. And there he saw the sight which he had been dreading all the last few days.

"I knew they would, the bloody swine!"

Gul'sary stood under an awning, with a bandage around his tail, tied up with a halter. Between his straddled hind legs there was a large, tightly inflamed swelling, the size of a small jug. The horse was standing motionless with his head in the manger. Tanabai groaned, bit his lip, wanting to go up to the pacer but not daring. He felt terrible, terrible with the emptiness of the stable, the empty yard and the lonely, gelded pacer. He turned away and hurried out. There was nothing that could be done, it was too late.

In the evening when they had got home again, back to the *yurta*, Tanabai said sadly to his wife, "My dream has been fulfilled."

"How?"

"I couldn't talk about it while we were visiting our friends. Gul'sary will never run away again. Do you know what they've done to him? They've gelded him."

"I know. That's why I made you go to the village. You were afraid of knowing about this and why? You're not a child. Is it the first and will it be the last time that a stallion has been gelded? It has always been like this and always will be. Everyone knows that."

Tanabai did not answer. He just said, "No, all this makes me feel that our new president is a wicked man. I feel it in my heart."

"That's nonsense, Tanabai," said Dzhaidar. "To say that, because they have gelded your pacer, the president is a wicked man. Why? He's new here. It is a big and difficult task. Choro said that now they are going into the problem of the *kolkhozes* and trying to help them. There are new plans for this. You are judging things too soon. There's a lot going on about which we know nothing . . ."

After supper Tanabai went out to the herd and was out there until long into the night. He cursed himself, trying to forget everything, but he could not get out of his mind the sight which he had seen that day in the stable. He thought as he rode round the herd. "Perhaps it was wrong to judge a man in this way. Stupid, of course. No doubt it's because I'm growing old, I spend all the year round with the herd, see nothing and know nothing of what's going on. But how long is life to be so hard? You hear speeches which sound as if everything is doing well. All right, perhaps I'm wrong. Please God that I am wrong. But there are, no doubt, others who think as I do."

Tanabai rode over the steppe, not finding an answer to his doubts. He remembered how they had started up the collective farm, their *kolkhoz*; how they had promised the people a happy life and how they had fought for the fulfilment of their dreams. They had turned everything upside down and dug over everything old. They had begun to live quite well; they would have lived even better if it had not been for that accursed war. And what about the present? Several years had passed since the war and still we were all patching things up on the *kolkhoz*, as if it

98

was an old *yurta*. You mend it in one place and it tears in another. Why? Because now it seemed as if the *kolkhoz* was not theirs to control, but someone else's. Once upon a time what they decided at a meeting was law. They knew that they had made the decision themselves and that they had to carry it out. But now the meetings were just empty chatter. No one was concerned about you. It was as if not the members of the *kolkhoz* controlled things, but someone from the sideline. As if it were easier to see from the sideline what needed to be done, how to do the work better and how to organise it. They alter things, first one way, then another and there is not the slightest change for the better. It was even strange when you talked to the people—they would ask at once, "Well, you are a party member, you tell us; you started the *kolkhoz*, you shouted loudest of all, you explain how it is that things are as they are now." What can one say to them? If only one could collect them together and talk things over. One could ask each man what he was thinking, what ideas he had, what troubles. But no, now representatives come from the regional centre but not even the old ones whom we knew; in the old days the representatives came and walked around and anyone could take up a matter with them. But now someone arrives, yells at the president in his office, but does not talk with the village soviet at all. They do speak at the party meetings, but much more about the international situation, as if the situation in the *kolkhoz* was not so important. All they say is just, "Work. Fulfil the plan!" and that's the lot.

Tanabai remembered how not long before someone had come and talked about some new language teaching.* When Tanabai had tried to talk with him about conditions on the *kolkhoz*, he had looked at him in an old-fashioned way. "Your thoughts," he said, "are questionable." He did not approve. How had all this come about?

"As soon as Choro gets from his bed," decided Tanabai, "I will get him to open his heart to me and I will do the same to him. If I'm mistaken let him tell me, and if not? No, it cannot be so. Of course I am wrong. Who am I but a simple old herdsman? People at the top are wiser."

Tanabai came back to the *yurta*, but he could not sleep. He

* No doubt based on Stalin's thesis on "Marxism and linguistics".

kept on racking his brains. What was the trouble? He just did not know.

He did not have his talk with Choro. He was up to his neck in work before he set off to wander with the herd.

Again the nomads moved off into the mountains for the whole summer, the whole autumn and winter until the next spring. Again the herds and the flocks went along the river and through the water meadows. The caravans of pack animals passed by. In the air were the sounds of different voices. The young girls in their bright scarves and dresses sang about the parting to come.

Tanabai drove his herd across the big meadow, over the hillocks by the village. That house, that yard which he had visited with his pacer was still there on the edge of the village. Now that woman was no longer his, nor was the pacer, Gul'sary. Everything had vanished into the past; that time had become silent, like the skeins of grey geese after the spring.

"The camel runs for many days, seeks and calls for its young one. Where are you, dark-eyed little camel? Answer me! The milk flows from my teats, from the full udder and flows down my legs . . . White milk . . ."

12

In the autumn of that year the fate of Tanabai Bakasov suddenly
changed.

Returning from over the hill, he had stopped in the foothills
on the autumn pastures, in order to get the herd up quickly to
the winter pastures in the mountains.

Just then a messenger arrived from the *kolkhoz*.

"Choro sent me," he said to Tanabai. "He asked me to tell you
to come to the village in order to go to a meeting at the regional
centre."

Next day Tanabai came to the *kolkhoz* office. Choro was there
in the *partorg's* room. He was looking much better than he had
been in the spring, although it was clear from his bluish lips and
gaunt appearance that he was still ill. He was, however, in good
form, very busy, with people all around him. Tanabai was glad
to find him better and that he was back at work.

When they were alone, Choro looked at Tanabai, touched his
sunken cheeks and said, with a smile, "Tanabai, you don't look
your age. How long is it since we saw one another, not since the
spring? *Kumys* and mountain air, that's what does you good!
But I'm dropping back a bit. Time, of course, passes . . ." Choro
was quiet for a moment and then started to talk business. "Look,
Tanabai. I know what you will say to this, give the impudent
fellow a spoonful and he will try to take five at a go. I'm asking
for your help again . . . Tomorrow we are going to a stockmen's
meeting. Things are bad in that sector of the work, especially
with the sheep rearing in our *kolkhoz*. In a word, we're in a mess.
The regional committee have put out the call— 'Communists
and *komsomols* out to the backward areas! To the flocks!'
Help us, just as you did with the horses; thank you for doing
that, and now help us again, take over a flock and become a
shepherd."

"Not so fast, how you rush on, Choro." Tanabai was silent as he thought to himself, "I'm used to horses and it will be dull with the sheep and how will all this work out?"

"I can twist your arm, Tanabai," said Choro, "and you can do nothing about it—it's a party task. Don't be angry. If you ever have to remind me, do it frankly and I will at once take the responsibility."

"I'll remind you so well, you won't thank me for it," Tanabai laughed, not realising that soon enough he would have to remind Choro about everything. "But about taking on a flock, I will have to talk that over with my wife."

"Well, think it over. But decide by tomorrow as we have to report before the meeting. You can consult Dzhaidar later and explain everything to her. I will find time, too, to go and tell her all about it. She's wise, she'll understand. If you hadn't had her behind you, you would have wrung your own neck long ago," joked Choro. "How is she? And how are the children?"

They talked on about families, illnesses, this and that. Tanabai all the time wanted to talk about the main matter with Choro, but the cattlemen, who had been called down from the mountains, began to look in and Choro, too, was in a hurry and kept glancing at his watch.

"Right then. Hand over your horse to the stable. You will all go tomorrow on the lorry. We've got a lorry now and there's a second one on the way. We're waking up. But I'll go now; I have to be in the regional committee offices by seven. The president is already there. I think I'll make it on the pacer by evening, he's as reliable as a car."

"What, you're riding Gul'sary now?" Tanabai was amazed. "So the president thinks well of you, eh?"

"Well or not, I don't know, but he gave him to me. You know we had some trouble," Choro laughed and waved his hand. "For some reason Gul'sary took to hating the president. Simply could not stand him. He would become wild and not let him get near. They tried, but it was no use, Gul'sary would die first. But I ride him; he's a wonderful mount, you schooled him well. You know, sometimes my heart is bad and painful, but when I sit on Gul'sary he starts off and seems to take the pain away. For this reason alone I'm ready to be *partorg* for the rest of my days. He keeps me fit." Choro laughed.

Tanabai did not laugh.

"I also dislike him."

"Who?" asked Choro, wiping the tears from his eyes.

"The president."

Choro became serious.

"Why do you dislike him?"

"I don't know; he seems to me to be an empty fellow, empty and cruel."

"I really don't know; you are hard to satisfy. You've reproached me all my life for being too gentle and now you don't like this man. I've only just started work under him; it's too early for me to judge yet."

They were silent. Tanabai had wanted to tell Choro about the chain fetters with which they had hobbled Gul'sary; how they had gelded the stallion, but it seemed to him now to be irrelevant, not convincing. In order not to prolong the embarrassing moments, Tanabai spoke of something more pleasant.

"It's very good that they've given us a lorry. It means they are giving some help to the *kolkhozes*. Not before time. Most necessary. Do you remember how, before the war, we got our first one-and-a-half tonner. Everyone came to the meeting we held. And why not, it was our own *kolkhoz's* lorry. You made a speech about it, 'Look, comrades, the fruits of socialism!' Later on they took it away to the war."

... Those were the days. A wonderful time, like the sunrise. Not only a lorry, either. When people returned from building the Chuisky Canal, they brought back gramophones with them! How the village enjoyed the new songs. That was the end of the summer. They'd get together in the evening at those houses which had gramophones and bring them out in the street and everyone listened to the record about the girl shock-worker in the red scarf. "Hey, you in the red scarf, make me some tea." That also was one of the fruits of socialism ...

"We were the same. Do you remember, Choro, after the meeting how we all crowded into the thirty-hundredweight, crammed full it was," Tanabai recalled, "I stood by the cab holding a red flag, as if we were on parade. We went just like that for the fun of it to the station and then along the railway to the next station over in Kazakhstan. We drank beer there in the park. And there and back we sang songs. Few of those *dzhigits* have survived, almost all were killed in the war. Yes and do you know, on the way back that night, I still stood there holding that red flag. I wouldn't let it go. Who could have seen it in the darkness? But I still held on to it, it was my flag. All the time I sang, I got quite hoarse, I remember. Why don't we sing now, Choro?"

"We're getting old, Tanabai, it wouldn't do."

"Yes, but I'm not talking about us, we have done with singing. Look, I visit my son at his boarding school. What does he learn there? He knows, of course, how to butter up those in charge. 'You, father,' he says, 'should bring some *kumys* more often to the director!' Yet he's getting on well enough with his studies. But you should hear how they sing. When I was working as a boy labourer at Yefremov's in Aleksandrovka, he once took me to the church at Easter. Well, our children stand on the stage, hands straight down the seams, fixed faces and they sing as people did long ago in the Russian church. All just the same; I don't like it. In general, there is a lot that I don't understand now; I would like to talk things over with you; I've got out of touch with life; I cannot understand everything that's going on."

"All right, Tanabai. We'll talk another time and choose a good time for it." Choro began to collect his papers into his case. "Only don't worry too much. For example, I believe strongly, that however difficult things are, we'll stand on our own feet and make our dreams come true." He was still speaking as he left the room. On the threshold he stopped and turned.

"Listen, Tanabai, I was going along the street not long ago and your house looks completely deserted. Don't you ever go and look at it? Of course you're all the time in the mountains and the house has no real master. Dzhaidar on her own during the war kept it better. You go and see and then tell us what has to be done and we'll help with repairs. Our Samansur came on holiday in the summer and couldn't wait when he saw it. He took his scythe, 'I'll go,' he said, 'and cut the weeds in Tanabai's yard.' Plaster has fallen down, windows are broken and the sparrows fly around the rooms as if it was a barn."

"You're right about my house. Please thank Samansur. How's he getting on with his studies?"

"He's in the second course now and is doing well. You say

'Look at youth', but I judge by my son. Modern youth is not too bad. From what he says they have some excellent young fellows at the institute. Well, we'll see later on. Youth is literate, and can think for itself . . ."

Choro went off to the stable and Tanabai went to look at his house. He went all round it. The dried weeds cut down by the student son of Choro were dusty and crackled under foot. His house indeed lacked the eye of its master. The other herdsmen had left relatives in theirs or arranged for them to look in. But his two sisters lived in other villages; he did not get on with his brother, Kulubai, and Dzhaidar had no close relatives at all. So it was that his house was neglected. Now he was off again on the wander, as a shepherd this time. Tanabai was still doubtful about the idea, but he knew that Choro would persuade him, he would not be able to refuse him and, as always, he would agree.

In the morning they drove out from the village to the regional centre. The new three-tonner Gaz delighted them all. "We're riding like the czars," joked the herdsmen. Tanabai was enjoying it—he had not travelled like this for a very long time, not since the war in fact. Then he had had to ride along the Slovakian and Austrian roads on American "Studebakers". They were powerful, three-axled lorries. "If only we had such lorries," Tanabai had thought then, "especially for carting the grain down from the foothills. They'd never get stuck." He had believed that once the war was over they would have them; after victory they'd have everything . . .!

In the open lorry in the wind, it was difficult to talk. All were quiet until Tanabai had said to the younger men.

"Give us a song, boys. What are you looking at us old men for? You sing, we'll listen."

The young men had sung, at first they took some time to get going, but then they were caught up in it. The journey was more fun. "That's good," thought Tanabai, "it's better. But best of all they have called us together at last. They'll give us a report how and what is to be done and what will happen on the *kolkhoz*. Our superiors know better. We only know the local picture. They will tell us, you'll see, and then we'll get to work again."

At the regional centre it was noisy with lots of people about. Lorries, carts and many horses filled the whole square around the club. The *shashlik* and tea sellers were there. Smoke, smells and shouts arose all around.

Choro was waiting to meet them. "Get out quickly and we'll go and get our seats. It'll begin soon; Tanabai, where are you off to?"

"Just a moment," called Tanabai, making his way through the crowd of horses. He had noticed Gul'sary from the truck and was going towards him. He had not seen him since the spring.

The pacer stood saddled among the other horses, but stood out from them with his bright yellow dun coat, his wide strong croup and his hook-nosed head with his dark eyes.

'Good morning, Gul'sary, good morning," Tanabai said quietly as he came up. "How are things with you?"

The pacer's eye turned and he recognised his old master, he stamped his feet a little and whinnied.

"You don't look too bad, Gul'sary. Why, you've put some weight on in the chest. You have a lot of running around, I expect. Things were bad at one time, weren't they. I know. But now you're in good hands. Behave well and everything will be all right." Tanabai felt the oats in the nosebag. "Choro doesn't let you go hungry. Well, you stay here and I'll be going along."

At the entrance to the club there was a bright banner hanging on the wall with the words "Communists, forward!" and "The Komsomol—the Vanguard of Soviet youth!"

There were many people crowding around in the foyer and in the hall itself. In the doorway Choro and the president, Aldanov, met Tanabai.

"Tanabai, come over here for a moment," said Aldanov; "we've already put you down. Here's your notebook. You must speak. You're a party member and our best herdsman."

"What am I to talk about?"

"Say that you, as a communist, have decided to go over to the backward sector of the *kolkhoz*, as shepherd to a flock of lambing ewes."

"Is that all?"

"Is that all? Tell them about your promises, tell them what tasks you are taking on. For instance, I swear before the party and people that I will rear a hundred and ten lambs from each hundred ewes and that I will shear three kilogrammes of wool from each sheep in the flock."

"How can I say that when I have not even seen the flock?"

"What next? You'll get your flock." Choro tried to smooth things over. "You'll be able to choose your sheep yourself, each one. Don't worry, and say also that you'll take two *komsomols* as shepherds under your control."

"Who?"

People were pushing around them as Choro consulted his list.

"Ashim Bolotbekov and Bektai Zarlykov."

"But I've never even spoken to them—what do they think?"

"Once again, off you go with your own ideas. You're a strange man. Isn't it all the same? They won't run away . We've already allotted them to you, it's all decided."

"Well, if it's all decided, why are you talking it over with me?" Tanabai walked off.

"Just a moment," Choro held him back, "you've remembered everything?"

"I've remembered, I've remembered," Tanabai answered irritably.

13

The meeting finished towards evening. The regional centre emptied; people went their way, some up to the mountains, others to the flocks and herds, to the farms, to the villages and the settlements.

Tanabai left with the others in the lorry, up the hill out of Aleksandrovka, across the steppe plateau. It was dark and windy. It was autumn. Tanabai huddled in a corner of the lorry and retreated with his thoughts into his turned-up collar. So the meeting was over. He himself had said nothing special, but had listened to the others. It seemed that there was a lot of work to be done to put everything right. That *oblast'* secretary in his spectacles was speaking the truth. "No one has prepared the road for us, we must make it for ourselves." From the thirties it had been first uphill, then downhill again. This matter of the *kolkhoz* farms was not an easy one. He himself already half grey-headed had squandered all his youth; he had seen and done so much and talked such nonsense, but all to no avail; there was no end to the difficulties with the *kolkhoz* . . .

Well, work means work. The secretary had spoken the truth when he had said that life will never run itself, as some of them had once thought after the war. One must always give it a shove as long as one lives. Life turns its rough side towards you and your shoulders get callouses on them. Never mind the callouses, your soul was happy when you were doing something, and so were the others who all drew happiness from their work in the end. How would he get on with a flock of sheep? What would Dzhaidar say about it? He hadn't even been able to drop into the shop and get some sweets for the girls. And he had made those promises. It was easy to say that one would rear a hundred and ten lambs out of every hundred ewes and three kilos of wool from each sheep in the flock. Each lamb would have to be born and reared but pitted against each were the rain, wind and cold. Take a wisp of wool, you cannot see it; blow on it and it isn't there. Where do the kilos come from? Oh, they're gold, those kilos. But, no doubt, the others have not the slightest idea either how all this will be achieved . . .

Yes, Choro had fixed him and confused him. "Speak," he had said, "Just a few words and only about your promises. Do not say anything else. I don't advise it." Tanabai had taken his advice and had obeyed. He had stood up on the platform, lost his nerve and had said nothing of what was in his heart. He had just burbled out the promises and sat down again. He was ashamed when he thought about it although Choro was satisfied. But why was he so cautious suddenly? Was it because of his illness or because he was no longer the top man in the *kolkhoz*? Why had he cautioned Tanabai? No, something had altered in him, he had changed. No doubt because all his life as president he had pulled the *kolkhoz* along and his superiors had done nothing but swear at him. He'd had to learn to be cunning, it seemed . . .

"You wait, my friend, I will remind you some time, face to face," Tanabai thought to himself as he wrapped himself a bit deeper in his sheepskin coat. It was cold and windy and there was still a long way to go. Was something else awaiting him at home?

Choro was riding home on the pacer. He was on his own, he had not waited for anyone else. He wanted to get home quickly as his heart was playing up. He let the horse go at his own speed; he had stood all day and now was running with his bold, accurate pacer's gait. His hooves sounded on the evening road like a machine. Out of everything he had known in the past, only his passion for running remained. Everything else had long ago died in him. They had killed it off so that all he knew now was the saddle and the road. Gul'sary lived for movement. He ran conscientiously and untiringly, as if he was going to recapture all that people had taken from him. He ran on but never reached that point.

Out in the wind and back in the saddle Choro found things easier. The pain in his heart had gone. On the whole he was pleased with the meeting. He had very much liked the speech of the *oblast'* secretary; he'd heard a lot about him, but this was the first time he had seen him. But all the same the *partorg* was not entirely satisfied. Something had jarred. He certainly wished Tanabai well. At such debates, meetings and conferences Choro was at his best, he knew where and what to say and what to leave unsaid. He was well apprised of this. But Tanabai, although he had done as Choro had said, had not wanted to understand. After the meeting he had said nothing to him. He had got into the lorry and turned his back. He had been upset. Oh, Tanabai, Tanabai, you're a simple man, life has taught you nothing, you know nothing and notice nothing. You have stayed just as you were in your youth. You want to strike everything down with a full blow from the shoulder. But times are changing. Now it is most important to know how and when to speak, and to be sure that one's words are in the spirit of the times, in tune with everyone else, not different, hesitating or stumbling, but as flowing as they were written down. Then all will be as it should be. But, Tanabai, if you do as you like, then the log will break and I will have to answer the questions, "How do you educate the members of your organisation? What sort of discipline is this? What is this laxity which you are permitting?" Oh, Tanabai, Tanabai . . .

I4

It was still that same night that had descended on them on their way. Old man and old horse. The fire was burning on the edge of the ravine. Every now and again Tanabai got up to adjust the coat that he had put over his dying Gul'sary. And again he went and sat by his head and (in his thoughts) went over his whole life. Years, years, years. Like the running of a pacer. And what had happened then in the late autumn of that year, in that early winter when he had been a shepherd with a flock . . .?

15

It was a dry and golden October in the mountains. Only on two days was there heavy rain, cold and mist. But then, during the night the weather changed, and in the morning as he came out of the *yurta*, Tanabai almost took a step back. The mountains seemed to be coming towards him with fresh snow on their tops. How fine they looked with the snow on them as they stood there, high in the sky in their virgin beauty, with their light and shade, as if God had only just created them! There, at the snow line, began a blue eternity. In its depth, in its far, far away blue was the clear transparent depth of space. Tanabai shivered from so much light and freshness and became wistful. Again he remembered the woman to whom he used to ride on Gul'sary. If the pacer had been at hand, he would have mounted him and shouting in delight and joy would have gone to her, appearing before her like this white morning snow.

But he knew that this was only a dream . . . Well, half of one's life is a dream, perhaps that's why life is so sweet. Perhaps life is precious to us because one's dreams lie just beyond fulfilment. He looked at the mountains and the sky and thought that everyone cannot be equally happy. Each life has its fate. In it are joys and griefs, just like the light and shade moving on a mountain at the same time. Life is full of that. "Perhaps she no longer waits for me? Or perhaps she also remembers as she sees the fresh snow on the mountains . . .?"

Man grows older, but his soul does not wish to give up, it still longs to stretch its wings and must have its say.

Tanabai saddled his horse, opened the sheep-fold and shouted into the *yurta* to his wife:

"Dzhaidar, I'm driving out the sheep. I'll return when you've done the housework."

The flock went off hurriedly a flowing stream of backs and heads as they climbed up the slope. The other shepherds from the near-by folds were also driving out their sheep. Here and there over the hillside, along the gullies and hollows wandered the flocks to collect the eternal gift of the earth—the grass. In greyish white huddles they went, standing out against the reds and browns of the autumn mountain grasses.

So far, so good. Tanabai had got a pretty good flock—ewes which had lambed two or three times already. Fifteen hundred head of them. Fifteen hundred anxieties. And after the forthcoming lambing, there should be over twice the number. But there was still a long time to go to the lambing season, to the shepherd's curse.

Life was quieter, of course, with the sheep than it had been with the horses, but Tanabai had taken some time to get used to them. Horses—that was a real job of work. But horse breeding had lost its importance, so they had told him. Lorries were taking their place. Horses, too, were no longer profitable. Now the important thing was sheep rearing, wool, meat, sheepskin. Such sober calculation offended Tanabai deeply although he realised that there was some truth in all this.

With a good stallion one could leave a herd of horses for a time, half a day or more and get on with other jobs. But with sheep this was impossible. You had to go everywhere with them by day and by night you had to guard them. In addition to the shepherd there should have been a herdsboy with the flock. But he had not been given one. So it was continuous work without relief, without rest. Dzhaidar had the job of night guard; during the day she could only go with their two daughters to take a look at the herd, but up to midnight she stood guard at the fold with a gun; after that he had to take over. But Ibraim, now in charge of all the animal breeding in the *kolkhoz*, could make excuses for everything.

"Where could I find you a herdsboy, Tanake?" he said with a dismal look on his face. "You know, all the young people are studying. Those who are not don't wish to hear anything about sheep; they are off to work in the town, on the railway or in the ore mines. I really do not know what to do. But you have just the one flock and you moan. But look at me! I have the whole stock breeding task lying on my shoulders. I'll be up in court about it! I was wrong to take this job on. Take people like your protégé

Bektai—he says to me that he wants me to be sure he has a radio, a cinema, a new *yurta* and the mobile shop to visit him once a week. 'If not, then you won't see me for dust.' You should have a word with him, Tanake . . ."

Ibraim was not lying. He regretted that he had attained such a position of responsibility. He was right, too, about Bektai. Now and again Tanabai found time to visit his *komsomol* protégés. Ashim Bolotbekov was an obliging lad, but not very efficient. Bektai, however, was handsome and quite good at this work, but in his black, slanting eyes there was an angry look. He greeted Tanabai sullenly and said, "Tanake, don't fly off the handle. You'd do better to stay with your children. I've enough people coming round to check up on me without you starting as well."

"What, would it make things worse for you?"

"No, no worse. But I don't like your type. People like you were always flattering, praising everything, hurrah, hurrah! But you yourselves have never seen a decent life and don't give us much of one either."

"Careful, young fellow." Tanabai could scarcely control himself and hissed through his teeth. "Don't poke at me with your finger. This is no business of yours. It was we who flattered and not you. And we are not sorry. We did it for you. If we hadn't, I would like to have seen you talking as you just have. Not only would there have been no cinema or papers for you; you wouldn't have known your own name. You would have had just one three-letter name—*kul*, or *rab*, slave!"

Tanabai did not like Bektai, although secretly he admired him for his straight talk He had some character but Tanabai was sorry that the boy was not really on the right track. Later on after they had parted they met by chance in the town, he had said nothing to him and had not listened to him.

* * *

That early winter . . .

It arrived quickly on its fierce white camel and caught out the forgetful shepherds. October had been dry and golden, but winter arrived all at once in November.

Tanabai had driven the sheep back to the fold one evening

114

and everything had seemed to be in order. But at midnight his wife woke him up:

"Get up, Tanabai! I'm completely frozen. It's snowing."

Her hands were cold and she had brought in a smell of wet snow; her rifle was wet and cold. Outside was a night of whiteness. The snow was falling heavily. The sheep in their fold were disturbed, shaking their heads at the strangeness, coughing, shrugging off the snow, yet still it came down and covered them. Tanabai drew his heavy coat around him. "Winter, you have come to visit us very early. What does it mean, good or bad? Perhaps you will ease up later on? If only you would go before the lambing. That's what we ask. But meanwhile do what you must. It's your right and you can do it without anyone's leave . . ."

The infant winter was silent, busily working on in the darkness, so that by morning everyone would gasp as they fussed and bustled about.

The mountains froze still as dark giants in the night. The winter meant nothing to them. It was the shepherds with their flocks who were worried. But the mountains would stand there as they will always stand.

That unforgettable winter had begun, but no one yet knew what it would get up to before it ended.

The snow settled; more fell a few days later, then more and more, until it drove the shepherds from the autumn pastures. The flocks began to move around to hide in the gorges, in the sheltered spots where there was less snow. The ancient art of the shepherds is to find fodder for their flocks in places others would brush aside, saying there was nothing there but snow. This was why they had become shepherds. Sometimes one of their superiors would come, look around a bit, ask a few questions, promise the earth and then quickly go down the mountains and away. The shepherd was on his own again, face to face with winter.

Al the time Tanabai was anxious to get down to the *kolkhoz* to make sure what they were thinking down there about the lambing; to see if everything had been stocked up and prepared in readiness. But how could he find time to get there? There was not a moment to breathe. Once Dzhaidar had gone down to see their son at the school but she did not stay long; she knew that it was very difficult for Tanabai to manage on his own. At that time Tanabai tended the flock with the help of their daughters. He put the little one in front of him on the saddle and drew the coat around her to warm her; she was warm and snug, but her sister froze as she sat behind her father. Even the fire at home seemed to burn differently, not at all cosily.

Their mother returned the next day to a great welcome. The children climbed on her neck and had to be pulled off by force. Yes of course Daddy is Daddy, but without Mother, even he is not the same.

Thus time passed by. The winter proved to be changeable— for a time it was cold and hard, then it eased off, suddenly there were two snow storms, then the wind relented and there was a thaw. This gave Tanabai a warning. It'd be all right if the lambing took place in a warm spell, but, if not, what then?

The bellies of the sheep became more and more heavy. Those carrying heavy lambs or twins began to sag. The ewes in lamb walked with difficulty, carefully, and were very weak because of their size. Their backbones stuck out. But no wonder, for the young were growing in the womb, filling out with their mother's gift, yet every blade of grass had to be forced out from under the snow. The shepherds should be giving them fodder morning and evening, fodder that should have been brought up to the mountains from the *kolkhoz,* but everything from down there in the barns was held up by the snowfall. There was nothing except seeds and oats for the working horses.

Every morning, as he drove the flock out of the fold, Tanabai inspected the ewes feeling their bellies and udders. He calculated that if all went well he would fulfil the plan as far as the lambs were concerned, but the wool would not be sufficient. The fleeces grew badly in the winter and on some of the sheep the wool was thinning and falling out. They should be better fed. Tanabai was worried and angry, but he could do nothing about it. He cursed himself roundly for obeying Choro. He had made some promises. He had got up and made his speech, "I am one of the progressives. I give my word before party and my country." If only he had not said that. And where did party and country come into it? Just a normal matter of farming. No, that was how it was laid down. "Why do we utter these words, necessary or not, at every turn?"

Of course he was to blame. He hadn't thought it over. He'd listened instead to the prompting of others. They would be able to lie their way out of it, but he was sorry for Choro. He was never lucky. One day he was fit, then he was ill for two. All his life he fussed around, persuaded and hoped, and what was the result? He was now careful and chose his words. Once he had got ill he should have retired.

So the winter went on, sometimes encouraging, sometimes alarming the shepherds. In Tanabai's flock two ewes died from starvation and complete exhaustion. His young shepherd protégés lost several each. But this was unavoidable as dozens of ewes were lost every winter. The main danger still lay ahead in what was to come later, just before the spring.

Suddenly it got warmer. At once the udders began to swell. There they were, those gaunt ewes, scarcely able to drag along their bellies and their pink teats were filling out not day by day, but hour by hour. How and where did the sheep get the nourishment? There was a rumour that already ewes had lambed in one of the other flocks. This was because the time of coming into season had not been properly noted, and was the first sign that in a week or two the lambs would be falling out like ripe pears. They would hardly have time to attend to all of the lambs. Then the shepherd's curse would begin. He would worry about every lamb and curse the day that he started to work with the flocks and, at the same time, his joy would be boundless if he saved the young lambs, if they managed to stand up on their own feet and flaunt their tails at winter.

But if only it would be like that, if only it would be so; so that one didn't have to hide and could look other people in the face.

They sent up some helpers from the *kolkhoz,* the *sakman-shchitsy*; these were usually elderly women or those with no children who could be persuaded to come out of the village to assist during the lambing period. Tanabai got two. They arrived complete with bedding, their tent and other things. Life became brighter, but of course, they really needed not two, but seven, in order to cope properly. Ibraim promised that they would get the extra help when the flocks got over to the lambing point, in the Valley of the Five Trees, but that meanwhile two would be enough.

The flocks moved off, descending to the foothills, on their way to the lambing points. Tanabai asked Ashim Bolotbekov to help the women to go down and get settled, while he drove down the flock. He saw them off in the morning, a whole caravan, and then he collected the sheep and let them take their time gently, so that it would be easy for the carrying ewes. He would then have to make this journey twice more to help the two younger men. The sheep went along slowly and did not want to be hurried. Even the dog got bored with his task and started running around from side to side. The sun was already setting, but there was still warmth in its rays. The lower the flock went into the foothills the warmer it became. Green shoots could be seen breaking through where the sun had warmed the soil. On the way there was a short delay while the first ewe lambed. This shouldn't be, thought Tanabai angrily as he blew out the ears and the nostrils of the new born lamb. The lambing was not due for a week at least, but here it was already.

Perhaps others would start lambing on the way. He looked round at them, but it did not seem likely. He calmed down a little at this and even cheered up at the thought of how pleased his little girls would be with the first lamb. A first one was always nice and this one was a particularly fine little fellow. White, with black eyelashes and black hooves. There were several ewes with fairly heavy fleeces—it was one of these which had lambed. The lambs from these ewes were always strong, born already with a little fleece, not like those from the thin-fleeced sort of ewe, which always produced almost bare lambs.

"Well, as you're in such a hurry, take a look around at God's world," said Tanabai. "Bring us luck! Bring us many more like yourself, so that there will be no room for our feet, and our ears may ring with your bleating and you will all survive." He lifted the lamb high above his head. "Look down, protector of the sheep. Here is our first-born, help us!"

The mountains stood all around in their silence.

Tanabai put the lamb under his coat and walked on his way,

driving the sheep. The ewe ran behind, bleating with concern about her young one.

"Come on, come on," Tanabai said to her, "he's here and he won't run away." The lamb soon dried under his coat and warmed up.

Tanabai got the flock down to the lambing point that evening.

Everything seemed set up, smoke was coming from the *yurtas*. The helpers were busy around their tent. Everything was under control. There was no sign of Ashim, but, of course, he had already taken the pack-camel and set off so that tomorrow he could bring his flock down. All was going well.

But what Tanabai then noticed shook him like a clap of thunder in a cloudless sky in the middle of the day. He had not expected anything wonderful, but he had not expected that the lambing shed would have a rotten, collapsed reed roof, holes in the walls, no doors or windows and that the wind would be howling through and through. All around there was practically no snow left, but there were drifts in the shed.

The sheep-fold, made long ago from rocks, also lay in ruins. Tanabai was so upset that he did not stop to see how the little girls greeted the lamb. He just gave it to them and went straight off to inspect everything. Wherever he looked there was the same neglect, such as the world had never seen. No doubt since the war everything had been left; somehow they had got through the lambing each year and had gone off leaving everything to the elements. On the roof of the barn there was a sad-looking crooked pile of rotting hay and a few broken bales of straw. This was all the feed and all the litter for the lambs and ewes of the whole flock. In addition there were two half-empty sacks of barley flour and a box of salt chucked in one corner. In the same corner there were also several lamps with broken glasses, a rusty can of paraffin, two spades and pitchforks. He felt like pouring paraffin over the lot, putting a match to it and letting the whole lot burn away to the devil dogs* while he himself went off into the blue, far away.

He walked around, stumbling over the frozen piles of last year's muck, mixed with snow. Words failed him. All he could do was

* In Asia the devil is said to appear in the form of a dog.

to repeat like a simpleton, "Is it possible? Is it possible? Is it possible?"

Then he rushed from the shed and hurried to saddle his horse. His hands shook as he did up the leathers. He would ride down to them, wake them all up and really start things moving. He would seize Ibraim, the president Aldanov and Choro by the neck; they could expect no mercy from him. Once they had treated him like this, they would get nothing from him. That's all there was to it.

"Stop it!" Dzhaidar had managed to seize the halter. "Where are you off to? Don't you dare! Get down and listen to me!"

What use was it to try to stop Tanabai now?

"Let go! Let go!" he shouted, straining at the halter, bearing down on his wife and beating the horse. "Let go, I tell you! I'll kill them! I'll kill them! I'll kill! . . ."

"I won't let you go. If you want to kill someone then kill me!"

The *sakmanshchitsy* ran up to Dzhaidar's aid and the little girls ran up, too, crying, "Father, Father, don't!"

Tanabai cooled down a bit but he was still ready to go.

"Don't stop me, don't you see the state of things here? Can't you see the ewes with their lambs? Where shall we put them? What about tomorrow? Where's the roof? Where's the fodder for them? They'll all die and who will be responsible? Let me go!"

"Wait, wait! If you do go what will happen? You'll shout and make a great scene and what will be the result? If they haven't done anything so far, it means that they have no resources. If they had any, of course the *kolkhoz* would have put up a new shed."

"But they could have repaired the roof at least, and where are the doors and windows? Everything is in ruins; there's snow in the shed, no one has mucked it out for at least ten years. See how much hay they've left and it's all rotten. Is that suitable for the lambs? Where do we get their litter from? Leave the lambs to die in the muck? Is that what you want? Get out of my way!"

"That's enough, Tanabai, be sensible! Are you any better than anyone else? We're all the same, and you are supposed to be a man!" His wife was trying to shame him. "You'd do better to think out what can be done here before it is too late. Spit on that lot down there! We are responsible and we must do something. I noticed a thick clump of dog-rose bushes back there by the track. They're prickly, of course, but we could cut them down and make a roof and pile manure on the top. For the litter we can cut rough grass. Somehow we'll fix things up unless the weather beats us."

The helpers joined in too, trying to calm Tanabai down. He got off his horse, spat with feeling and emphasis and went into the *yurta*. He sat there with his head bowed, drooping as if after a serious illness.

All the family was quiet. They were afraid to say a word. Dzhaidar took the kettle off the dung fire and made some really strong tea; she brought water in a jug and gave it to her husband to wash his hands. She laid a clean table cloth, found some sweets and put slices of butter on a dish. They invited in the two helpers and began to drink the tea.

Women! They sit there drinking their tea as if they are at a tea-party. Tanabai didn't say a word, but after he had drunk his tea, went out and began to reconstruct the collapsed stone wall of the sheep-fold. It was slow work. But they had to have somewhere to drive the flock for the night. The women came out and also got to work with the stones. Even the little girls tried to carry them up.

"Run inside," said their father.

He was ashamed. He dragged the stones, not looking up. Choro had told the truth—but for Dzhaidar, Tanabai would have lost his head completely.

16

Next day Tanabai went to help the two young men bring down their flocks and then he worked for a whole week at a stretch. He could not remember a time like this—except at the front when they had worked for days on end preparing defences. But then there had been the whole regiment, the division, the army. Here there were just his wife, himself and only one of the women helpers for the other had to be with the sheep near-by.

The worst job was clearing out the muck from the shed and cutting and carrying the dog-rose bushes. The latter were thick and full of prickles. Tanabai's boots were torn, his old army tunic was in shreds. They tied the branches with cord and dragged them along. It was impossible to load them on to a horse or carry them by hand because of the prickles. Tanabai sent everything to the devil in his curses—it's called the Valley of the Five Trees and there's not even five stumps left. Bent treble, soaked in sweat, they dragged the damned dog-rose branches along, making a track up to the shed. Tanabai was sorry for the women but he could do nothing. They were working against time and hastily. He kept on looking up at the sky to see what was in store. If snow was to fall, then all they had done would be to no purpose. He kept sending the elder daughter to the flock to see if the lambing had started.

The work with the manure was even more of a trial. There was so much of it that it would take six months to move it all out. When compressed sheep dung is kept dry under cover, it is pleasant stuff to work with. The cut out layer comes away in a solid, firm slice. It is put to dry in big stacks. The warmth from burning sheep dung is pleasant and it burns clearly, golden; shepherds keep warm with it all winter. But if it has been lying under the rain and snow as it was in the shed, then there is nothing so heavy to cart around or dig. It is hard labour to work it and for them time would not wait. During the night they lit their smoky lamps and continued to carry out this cold, sticky, leaden muck. They had already spent two days on the work.

Outside they had already made a huge pile of it but there was still no end to the work. They hurried to clear just one corner of the shed for the expected lambs. But what did one small corner mean? It was small indeed for this big herd, to take all the ewes and their young. Some twenty to thirty lambs would arrive each day. 'What will happen?' was Tanabai's sole thought as he piled the muck on to the barrow, carried it out, came back again and went on without stopping until midnight or dawn. He felt sick. His hands were numb and the lamps kept on going out. It was good that their women helpers did not grumble; they worked as hard as Dzhaidar and Tanabai.

A day passed, another, and still they were carting the muck out; they had filled up some of the holes in the walls and the roof was done. One night as he was taking a barrow from the shed, Tanabai heard a lamb's bleat in the sheep-fold then its mother's answering call and the thumping of her feet. "It's started!" His heart thumped too.

"Did you hear that?" Tanabai called to his wife. At once they put down their barrows of dung, seized a lamp each and ran out to the fold. Holding high the flickering lamps, they looked the flock over. Where was the lamb? Over there in the corner! The ewe was already licking the tiny, shivering body of the new-born creature. Dzhaidar picked up the lamb and put it in a fold of her skirt. It was as well that they had got there in time so that the lamb had not frozen in the sheep-fold. Alongside they found another ewe with twins. Tanabai covered them with his coat. Five more ewes were in labour and were making a stifled lowing noise. It had begun. By the morning these would have given birth. They called out the two helpers. They started to drive out the ewes in labour to the corner of the shed which they had cleared out.

Tanabai laid down straw by the wall, put on it the lambs which had had the first colostrum from the ewes, and covered them with a sack. It was cold. He then put in the ewes. He stood there, biting his lip. But what was the use of thinking? All that was left was to hope that, perhaps, everything would work out somehow. What a lot there was to be done, to worry over. If only there had been enough straw, but there was not. Ibraim would give a convincing reason even for that deficiency. He would say, "Try to bring straw across trackless country into the mountains!"

Well, what will be, will be. He fetched the tin with the dissolved ink in it. On the single lamb he put a figure "2" and on each of the twins a "3" and similarly for their mothers. "Otherwise how could you sort them out when they start arriving in their hundreds? It's here all right, no longer in the future, the shepherd's curse is with us now."

It had begun sharply, cruelly, just as when you're defending a position with no weapons and tanks are advancing. You crouch in your trench but do not run away, because there's nowhere to run to. You've two choices, either to survive the battle by a miracle or to die.

Tanabai stood that morning on the hillock before the flock was driven out to pasture and quietly looked around as if weighing up his position. His defence was ramshackle, useless. But he had to stay there; he, too, had nowhere to go. There was just the small winding little valley with its shallow stream between the sheltering cliffs; beyond them were higher hills, and beyond them others still higher and under snow. Above the white slopes were the bare rock faces, and there on the summits covered in solid ice, lay winter. Only a short way away. Only a slight change and down would come the clouds to the little valley and drown it in mist and you wouldn't find it.

The sky was grey, in a grey silent mistiness. The wind was blowing down off the mountains. All around was deserted. Mountains all around. Fear made Tanabai cold inside. In the ruined shed lambs were bleating. They had just had to drive ten ewes from the flock and leave them in the shed to lamb.

The rest went off quietly in search of the meagre grass. Out on the pasture now you had to have all your wits about you or a ewe which may have shown no signs that her time had come would suddenly lie down behind a bush and that was that! If you didn't keep your eyes open, the lamb would chill on the damp earth and become just a corpse.

However, Tanabai stood a while on the hillock, then with a resigned wave of his hand he went to the shed. There was still a mass of work to be done, if only they could succeed in getting it finished.

Later Ibraim arrived, he had brought some flour . . . his eyes were shameless. "And where," he asked, "shall I find these palaces you want? These sheds in the *kolkhoz* have been like this for years and so they remain. There are no others. We have not yet reached the era of communism."

Tanabai could scarcely restrain himself from flying at Ibraim with his fists threshing.

"What are these cracks for? I'm talking about work; I'm thinking about work. I have to take the responsibility . . ."

"Don't you realise that I'm thinking too? You are responsible for just the one flock and I'm responsible for the whole stock breeding task and results. So you think it's easy for me?" Suddenly, to Tanabai's great amazement this cunning fox burst into tears, hiding his face in his arms. Then he mumbled through his tears, "I'll be put on trial because of this. I'll be up in court. You can't get anything anywhere. People don't even want to come and work as helpers, not even for a short time. Kill me, torture me, I can do no more. Don't expect anything from me. I was foolish, foolish to take on this post . . ."

With these words he left, leaving the simple Tanabai not a little embarrassed. They were never to see him up there again.

The first hundred ewes had lambed. In Ashim's and Bektai's flocks higher up the valley, the lambing had not yet begun but Tanabai already felt that a catastrophe was about to strike them. All of the three adults—one could not count the elder helper who had to spend all her time out with the flock—and the elder girl were hardly able to keep up with the work of tending the births, wiping the lambs, putting them to the ewes, warming them with what they could find, mucking out and bringing in the coarse grass for the litter. But already the hungry cries of the lambs were to be heard and there was not enough milk for the ewes had nothing to give to them. What was ahead?

The shepherds' days and nights passed in a whirl, the lambing was right on top of them, not a second to sigh or even straighten their aching backs.

Yesterday the weather had given them a fright. All at once it turned cold. Lowering clouds had come upon them and hard, hail-like snow had fallen. Everything was lost in mist as it became dark.

But suddenly the clouds had broken up and it began to get warmer. There was a whiff of spring damp in the air. "Perhaps, please God, spring has come. But it must come properly—there's nothing worse than if it hovers around and then goes away again." Such were Tanabai's thoughts as he carried out some straw and afterbirth on a fork.

Spring came indeed, but not as Tanabai had expected. It came suddenly, during the night with rain, mist and sleet. In all its wet and cold it descended upon the shed, the *yurta,* the fold and on everything around. Streams and puddles were all over the slushy earth. Rain streamed in through the rotten roof, down the walls and filled the shed with a flood, making its inhabitants shiver to the marrow. It spurred everyone into action. The lambs were huddled together in the water, the ewes bleated loudly giving birth as they stood there. Spring was christening the young with cold water almost before they were born.

People rushed around in their coats with torches. Tanabai ran about. Like a pair of terrified animals his great boots splashed around in the darkness through the puddles and mire. The flaps of his coat beat around like the wings of some vast bird. He croaked and shouted at himself and the others.

"Pass me that crowbar at once! Now the spade! Some muck over here. Keep back the water!"

They had to divert to one side the streams of water now pouring into the shed. He cut the frozen earth, dug out some ditches.

"Give us some light here! Here! What are you standing and just looking for?"

The night was misty. Sleet was falling heavily. Nothing would stop it.

Tanabai ran into the *yurta* and lit the lamp. Here too everything was dripping but it was better than in the shed. The children were asleep and their blanket was beginning to get soaked. Tanabai gathered them up in his arms and dragged them and their bed into a corner, making a bit of space. He threw a roof sheet over the children so that rain didn't fall on them from above and ran out shouting to the women in the shed, "Bring the lambs into the *yurta*!" And he also ran to get some.

But how many could they squeeze into the *yurta*? A few dozen of them, perhaps, but no more and what about the rest? But they had to save as many as they could.

By now it was already morning. There was no end to the downpour. It eased a bit and then again there was rain, snow, rain and snow . . .

The *yurta* is crammed with lambs which bleat continuously. Stink, stench. The family have put all their things into one corner, covered them with a tarpaulin and have themselves all moved into the tent with the two helpers. The children are frozen and crying.

The shepherd's black days have come indeed. He curses his lot, all and everything in the world. He does not sleep or eat but uses up all his strength amongst the sheep, sodden from head to hoof, amongst the lambs stiffening with cold. Death is already reaping her harvest in the shed. Nothing stops her; she slips in where she will, through the roof, through the paneless windows and the doorless entrances. She appears and cuts down the lambs and their weakened mothers. The shepherd carries out the little blue corpses and piles up several of them beside the shed. On the track, in the fold, stand the heavy ewes, under the soaking rain and snow. They will lamb any time now. The rain beats down on them and their jaws shake from the cold. Their wet fleece is matted in soaked lumps . . .

The sheep no longer want to go out to pasture. What can they find out there in the cold and damp? The old *sakmanshchitsa* with a sack over her head drives them out from the fold but they run back as if to a paradise. The woman weeps, collects them together and drives them out again, and again they run back. Tanabai runs out in a white rage. He would like to take a stick to those silly sheep, but they are ewes in lamb. He calls the others and together they manage to get the flock out to the pasture . . .

From the time that this disaster began, Tanabai had lost all count of time, all count of the young dying before his eyes. Mostly they were twins, but sometimes triplets were born and all this wealth was being lost. All their work was in vain. The lambs were appearing and that same day were dying in the morass, in the mire and liquid muck. Those who remained coughed, wheezed and uncontrollably befouled each other. The ewes who had lost their young bleated, ran, shoved and trampled on those who were lying in labour. In all this there was something unnatural and hideous. Oh, how Tanabai wished that this process of birth could somehow be slowed down. He wanted to shout at these silly sheep, "Stop! Don't give birth! Stop!"

But the ewes, as if caught up in some dreadful plot, lambed one after the other, one after the other.

There arose in his heart a dark, terrible rage; it rose covering his eyes with a black mist of hate towards everything that was happening, towards the rotten shed, the sheep, himself, his life, towards everything for which he was struggling here like a caught fish beating against the ice.

A sort of torpor descended on him. His thoughts made him sick; he put them from him, but they would not go, they crawled back into his heart, into his head.

"What is all this for? What good is it to anybody? Why do we breed these sheep if we cannot keep them alive and protect them? Who is to blame? Who? Answer me, who? You and those like you, who talk too much. We boast that we will improve everything, catch up, overtake, and give our word to do so! We speak fine words. Well, now try and raise up the dead lambs! Rescue them! Drag out that dead ewe who's died in the puddle. Show the sort of person you are."

Especially at night splashing about, up to his knees in muck and urine, Tanabai was stifled by his dreadful, bitter thoughts. Oh, those sleepless nights of the lambing time! Under your feet the morass of rotten muck, above the rain pouring down. The wind blows through the shed as if it were an open field and blows out the lamp. Tanabai goes around by feels, falls down, crawls on all fours so as not to crush the new-born, finds his lamp and relights it and sees in its glimmer his black, swollen hands smeared with blood and dung.

It was a long time since he had looked at himself in a mirror. He did not know that he had turned grey and had aged by many years. Now indeed he could be called an old man. But he had no time to bother about that or about himself. There was no time to eat or wash. He allowed neither himself nor the others any rest. Seeing that things were heading towards a complete catastrophe, he got the younger woman helper on to the horse.

"Ride and find Choro. Tell him that he should come at once. If he won't come, then tell him that he need not show himself in front of me again."

She was back again by evening, fell out of the saddle, blue with cold and soaked to the skin.

"He's ill, Tanake. He's in his bed, but he said that in a day or two, even if he's dying, he'll come."

"May he not recover from this illness!" Tanabai cursed.

Dzhaidar wanted to check him, but she did not dare, she just could not.

The weather became brighter on the third day. The clouds dragged over the sky, mist rose in the mountains. But it was now too late. The ewes in lamb during those days had starved to such a degree that it was awful to see them. They stood there like wraiths, with vast bellies on thin legs. What sort of suck would they be able to give? What chance had they and the lambs which were still alive to live through to the summer and recover with the green grass? Sooner or later they would fall ill. If not, there would be *khurda,* wasting, with neither wool nor meat on them ...

Once the weather was better, another trouble came—the melted snow froze on the ground as clear ice. But at midday it had melted. Tanabai was glad; he might be able to rescue something from the wreck. Once again spade, forks and barrow went into action. They couldn't do much but they had to make paths to the shed, for otherwise it was impossible to walk a step. But they couldn't spare much time. They had to feed the suckling orphans and put them to ewes who had lost their own lambs, but they do not give in or accept other lambs easily. The lambs push and ask for milk. They take hold of fingers with cold lips and suck. If you drive them away, they will suck at the edge of your coat. They want food. They run after you in a bleating procession.

Cry or burst! How much more could he ask from these women and from the little girl? They could hardly stand. How many days is it now that their coats have not dried on them. Tanabai says nothing to them. Only once was he unable to control himself. The elder helper had driven the flock into the fold at midday as she wanted to help Tanabai. He came out to see how things were going. He looked and just boiled over with rage; the sheep stood there chewing at one another's fleece. This meant that the herd was threatened with death from famine. He ran out and yelled at her:

"What are you doing, old woman? Don't you see what's going on? Why didn't you say anything? Get out again! Drive out the flock and don't let them stop! Don't let them eat each other's wool! Don't let them stop for a minute or I'll kill you!"

Then came another trouble. One ewe with twins began to reject her own lambs. She butted them, would not let them come to her and kicked them. But the lambs crawled up, fell down and cried. This sort of thing happens when the cruellest law of self-preservation comes into force—when a mother refuses to suckle her own young, so that she herself may survive. This is contagious, like a disease. Just one ewe has to start it and then the others follow suit. Tanabai got really alarmed. He and his daughter drove the ewe, maddened with hunger, from the *yurta* into the sheep-fold and began to force her to feed her young. At first Tanabai held the ewe and his daughter brought the lambs up to her. But the ewe struggled and wriggled and tried to get free. The little girl had no success.

"Father, they cannot suck."

"They can, you're just hopeless."

"No, really, look, they're falling." She was almost in tears.

"You hold the ewe, I'll do it myself."

But what strength has a little girl? He had only just brought the lambs to the teats and they were just starting to suck, when the ewe gave such a wrench that the little girl fell over and off ran the sheep. Tanabai's patience gave way. He slapped the little girl. Never before had he hit one of the children, but this had been too much. The girl snivelled and he walked away. He spat and walked off.

He walked around and did not know how to ask forgiveness of his little daughter, but it was she who ran up to him:

"Father, she's feeding them! Mama and I brought the lambs to her and she's no longer chasing them away."

"That's fine, little one. You are a clever girl!"

At once his heart was lighter, as if all was not so bad. Perhaps they would succeed in saving what was left. Perhaps the weather would be better now, and all at once the shepherd's dark days might be over?

Again he got back to work. To work, work and work—only in that lay a chance to save everything . . .

A census-taker arrived—a boy on horseback. At last someone had come. He asked how things were. Tanabai would gladly have told him where to go, to whom and what to do . . . What business of his was it to ask questions?

"Where have you been before?"

"What do you mean, where? Around the flocks. I could not come earlier. I'm on my own."

"How are the others getting on?"

"No better than you. These three days have finished off many animals."

"What do the shepherds have to say about it?"

"What indeed! They curse. Some won't even speak. That Bektai just threw me out. He's so angry that you can't get near him."

"Yes . . . yes. I have had no chance to get to see him. But perhaps now I'll be able to. Well, and what are you doing?"

"Me? I'm taking a census."

"But are we going to get any help?"

"Yes. Choro, they say, has got out of bed. He sent a cart with hay and straw; they took everything from the stables—let them, he said, it'll be better if the horses die. But they say the cart got stuck somewhere—the roads are so bad."

"Roads! Why didn't they think about them earlier? It's always the same with us. What use will that cart be now? Well, I'll get to them!" Tanabai was threatening. "Don't ask any questions. Go and see for yourself, look, count, write it down. It's all the same to me now." Breaking off, he went into the shed to deal with the lambing. That day a further fifteen ewes were due to lamb.

Tanabai was walking out, collecting and cleaning up the afterbirth and noticed that the census-taker was pushing a paper in front of him.

"Sign the paper about the losses."

He signed without looking. He pressed so hard that the pencil broke.

"Good-bye, Tanake. Can I take any message?"

"I've nothing to say." Then he called the boy back. "Look in at Bektai's place. Tell him I'll somehow get to him by dinner time tomorrow."

Tanabai had no need to worry. Bektai was to beat him to it and arrive himself . . .

That night the wind got up and there was some snow, not very thick, but by morning the earth had a white covering. It fell on the sheep standing all night in the fold. They did not lie down but gathered into a huddle and stood, motionless and indifferent to everything. The shortage of food had gone on too long, for too long spring had fought with winter.

It was cold in the shed. Snowflakes fell through holes in the roof made by the rain, and whirled round in the lamp beam falling on to the freezing ewes and lambs. Tanabai was busy all the time, doing his duty like a soldier on a burial party after the slaughter on a battlefield. He was already used to his heavy thoughts, his anger had changed to silent rage. It was like a stake in his heart, he could not bend. He walked around, his boots squelching in the mire and he kept on going back to his past in those night hours.

Long ago he had been a shepherd boy. With his brother Kulubai, he had tended the sheep of one of their relatives. A year passed and it then transpired that they were working just for their food. The owner of the sheep had deceived them and did not want to discuss the matter, so off they went with their worn-out shoes, their pitiful rucksacks on their backs, empty-handed. As they left Tanabai threatened the man:

"I'll remember you for this when I grow up."

But Kulubai said nothing. He was five years older and knew that you couldn't frighten a master in that way. It would be better to become a boss oneself; to get some cattle, to lease land.

"When I become a boss, I'll never insult a worker," he said, even then.

They parted company that year. Kulubai became a shepherd to another *bai* and Tanabai went to Aleksandrovka to work for a

Russian settler, Yefremov. He was not very rich; he had a pair of oxen, two horses and a ploughed field on which he grew grain and he took the wheat to a rolling mill in the small town of Aulia-Ata. He worked himself from dawn to dusk, while Tanabai chiefly looked after the oxen and the horses. His master was stern but fair. He paid the proper wages. The poor Kirgiz of those days, always oppressed by their richer fellows, preferred to work for Russians. Tanabai learnt to speak Russian and travelling with the driver and being in that little town of Aulia-Ata, he saw a little of the world. Then came the revolution and turned everything upside down. The time had come for the Tanabais of this world.

Tanabai returned to the village. Another life began. It seized hold of him, carried him off and turned his head. All had come at once—land, freedom and rights. He was given farm work to do and it was at that time that he first got to know Choro. Choro was educated and taught the young people to write and spell. Tanabai badly needed to be literate, after all he was a farm worker. He joined a young communist cell and so did Choro. They then joined the party together. All went on at its own pace but the poor were now on top. When collectivisation began, Tanabai went into that wholeheartedly. He, as no one else, had to fight for a new life for the peasants so that all would become common property—land, cattle, work and dreams. Down with the *kulaks*! A difficult and stormy time started. By day—in the saddle, by night—at conferences and meetings. Lists of *kulaks* were drawn up. *Bais, mullahs*, all sorts of rich men were thrown out like weeds from a field. It was necessary to clear out the field so that other plants could grow. Among those in the lists was Kulubai. During the time that Tanabai had been busy at his meetings and conferences, his brother had come up in the world. He had married a widow and his farm had prospered. He had stock—sheep, a cow, two horses, a milking mare and foal, a plough, a harrow and so on. He hired workers for helping with the harvest. One couldn't say that he was rich, but he certainly was not poor. He lived well, but he also worked hard.

At the conference in the village soviet, when Kulubai's name came up, Choro said, "Let us consider this case, comrades. Shall we treat him as a *kulak* or not? Someone such as Kulubai could be useful to us in the collective. He came from peasant stock and does not indulge in hostile propaganda."

Various opinions were expressed, some for, some against, it was Tanabai's turn to speak. He sat there puffed up like a raven. Although he was only his step-brother, he was still his brother, and he would have to be against his brother. They lived in peace, although they rarely met one another. Each minded his own business. If he asked them to leave him alone, then how should he act in other cases, a protector or friend can be found for anyone. But if he said that they should decide without him, then they would think that he was avoiding the issue.

Everyone waited to see what he would say. Because he knew they were waiting, hardness of heart got the upper hand.

"Choro, you were always like this," he said as he got up. "They have written about bookworms in the papers—what do they call them?—'entellectuals'! You're also an entellectual. You're always having doubts, you're afraid that something will not be quite right. Why doubt? Once he's on the list—it means he's a *kulak*. No mercy! For the sake of Soviet rule, I wouldn't spare my own father. Don't let the fact that he's my brother worry you. I, not you, will be throwing him out as a *kulak*."

Kulubai came to see him the next day. Tanabai greeted him coldly without giving his hand.

"Why are you treating me as a *kulak*? Didn't we work together as labourers? Wasn't it us that the *bai* threw out?"

"That doesn't count now. You yourself have become a *bai*."

"What sort of a *bai* am I? I've gained all I have by my own hard work. I'm not ashamed. Take it all away from me, but why count me as a *kulak*? Fear God, Tanabai!"

"I'm not worried. You are one of the class enemy. We have to liquidate you in order to build up the collective farm, the *kolkhoz*. You're in our way and we have to throw you off our road . . ."

That was the last time they had talked together. It was already twenty years since they had last exchanged a word. There had been much discussion and many judgements when Kulubai was sent to Siberia.

All kinds of things were said. They even thought up a story that when Kulubai was taken from the village guarded by two mounted militiamen, he left with his head bowed looking at no one and saying good-bye to no one. When they had left the village and were going across the fields, it was said that he ran into the young wheat, the *kolkhoz*'s first winter wheat, and began to tear it up by the roots, to trample it down and crush it like an animal. The guards had to drag him away by force. As he left, so they said, he wept bitterly and cursed Tanabai.

Tanabai did not easily believe all this, "They want to scare me with their malicious gossip. But two devils to them, I won't give way." So he convinced himself.

But once, just before they harvested the crop, he went to the fields. The wheat had grown well that year, ear after ear was proudly waving, until he came to the place in the wheatfield where Kulubai had struggled in his despair, where he had trampled and torn up the young plants by the roots. All around the wheat stood high, but in that place it was just as if bulls had fought there; all was trampled, broken down, dried and overgrown with weeds. As he saw this, so Tanabai reined in his horse.

"Oh, you swine!" he whispered, boiling with rage. "You lifted your hand against the *kolkhoz*'s grain. That means you are indeed a *kulak*. And who more than you?"

He stood there a long time, silent and grim in thought, then turned and rode off without looking back. After this he avoided that place for a long time until they had finished the harvest and the stubble was flattened by the hooves of the cattle.

There were few then who spoke up in defence of Tanabai, most criticised him.

"God forbid that one should have such a brother. Better to have no relations at all." Some said this to his face. Yes, at that time people avoided him. Not openly, but when there was a question of voting for him to take such and such a post, they just abstained. Thus he was gradually eased out of active political work. Although he had convinced himself that the *kulaks* had burnt the collective farms, and had fired shots, he knew the truth that the *kolkhoz* was recovering and things were getting better. An entirely new life was starting. No, they'd not acted in vain.

Tanabai could remember all that, so long ago, in minute detail. It was as if all his life had stood still there at that wonderful time when the *kolkhoz* had gathered strength. Again he could remember the song about the girl shock-worker in the red scarf; he could remember the first thirty hundredweight and how he had stood by its cabin that night holding the red flag.

Tanabai wandered all night around the shed, doing his dreadful duty, thinking his dreadful thoughts. Why was everything giving way at the seams now? Perhaps they had made a mistake? Taken the wrong road? No, it couldn't be that. They were on the right road. What had happened then? Had they got lost? Gone off the road? When and how had this happened? Now there is this competition—they have written down what you have to do and it is of no concern to anyone how you will get on. Earlier there were red and black boards, each day so many discussions, arguments—who was on the red board, who on the black—this was important for people. No they say that all this was in the past and outdated. What is in its place? Empty discussions, promises. And nothing comes of them. Why? Who is to blame for all this?

Tanabai was tired from his endless thought. Indifference, torpor seized him. His work slowed down. His head ached, he longed for sleep. He saw how the younger helper was leaning against the wall. He saw how her reddened eyes were beginning to close as she was trying to fight off sleep and how she gradually slipped down and then sat on the ground, falling asleep with her head on her knees. He did not wake her. Then he too leaned against the wall and also began to slip down and could do nothing about it; his shoulders gave way under heaviness which pushed him down and down . . .

He awoke to a muffled shout and a heavy thud on the ground. The frightened sheep ran against his legs. He jumped up, not knowing what had happened. It was already light.

"Tanabai, help me, help!" his wife was calling.

The helper ran to her aid with him. He could see that a rafter falling from the roof had pinned her down. One end had slipped out of the collapsing wall and the rafter had given way under the weight of the rotted roof. All his sleepiness vanished.

"Dzhaidar!" he shouted and putting his shoulder under the beam he made a great effort and lifted its weight off.

Dzhaidar crawled out groaning. The women gathered around and felt her. Tanabai pushed them aside, not realising from fright what might have happened and felt under his wife's pullover with trembling hands.

"What's up? What's happened?"

"Oh, my back! My back!"

"What, is it bruised? Let me help."

He took off his coat, laid Dzhaidar on it and carried her from the shed. They examined her in the tent. There was nothing to be seen on the surface, but she had had a nasty blow and could not move.

Dzhaidar burst into tears.

"Why should this happen now of all times, and to me? Who will look after you?"

"Oh God," thought Tanabai. He was glad that she was alive. But what might this lead to? The work can go to all the devils. "My only wish is that you get well, my poor little one."

He began to stroke her head.

"Calm down, Dzhaidar. The main thing is for you to get well. Nothing else matters, we'll get by somehow."

All of them, now coming to their senses, began to try to cheer up and calm Dzhaidar. Indeed she herself began to feel better and smiled at them through her tears.

"It's better now. But don't be angry that it happened. I won't lie around. In two days I'll be up and about, you'll see."

The women got her bed made and lit the fire and Tanabai went back to the shed, scarcely able to believe that the accident had done nothing worse.

It was a white morning beneath new soft snow. In the shed Tanabai found a ewe crushed by the rafter which he had not noticed before. A sucking lamb was pushing at the teats of its dead mother. It seemed even more frightening and even more wonderful to Tanabai that his wife was alive. He took the little orphan and went to find it a foster mother. Then he put a post under the beam and another to buttress the wall, all the time wanting to go and see how his wife was. As he went out of the shed he saw a flock of sheep slowly wandering across the snow.

137

What strange shepherd was driving them on to his land? What flock is it? Why is he driving them here? The sheep should not be mixed up at this time. Tanabai went out to warn this straying shepherd that he had got into another's territory.

As he got closer he could see that the stranger was Bektai.

"Hi, Bektai, what are you doing?"

The other did not answer, but drove his flock on, striking the sheep with a crook. "Lambing ewes, too!" Tanabai was furious.

"Where have you come from? Where are you going? Good morning."

"From where you won't find me any more—and where I am going—you will see for yourself."

Bektai came towards him; he was wearing round his waist a belt of cord with his gloves stuck under his coat.

He held the crook behind his back and stopped a few paces away, but gave no greeting. He spat angrily and crushed the spittle into the snow. He raised his head. His young, handsome face was black with a heavy growth of beard. His lynx-like eyes looked full of hate and challenge. He spat again, brandished the crook and waved it in the direction of the flock.

"Take it. Count them if you like. Three hundred and eighty-five head."

"What?"

"I'm off!"

"What do you mean 'I'm off'? Where to?"

"Anywhere."

"What am I to do about it?"

"You're my chief."

"Well. What? Wait, wait, where are you going to?"

Only now did Tanabai realise what his protégé shepherd intended. He felt stifled and hot from the blood racing to his head. "How can you?" he said.

"Just like this. I've had enough. I'm fed up, right up to the neck with this sort of life."

"Do you know what you're saying? Your ewes will be lambing any moment. How can you?"

"I can indeed. Once they treat us like this, we can pay them back in the same coin. Good-bye!"

Bektai whirled the crook around his head in a circle and let it fly off and walked away.

Tanabai was frozen to the spot. He was speechless, as the other walked off without a backward glance.

"Think about it, Bektai!" he ran after him. "You can't do this. Think what you're doing! Do you hear?"

"Go away." Bektai turned round sharply. "You do some thinking. I want to live like people should. I'm no worse than anyone else. I can find work in the town and earn a wage. Why should I get lost out here with these sheep? Without fodder, without a lambing shed or even a *yurta* over my head. Get away! Go and flatter them and sink in the muck. Look at yourself—look at what you've become. You'll die out here soon enough. That's nothing to you. But you threw out challenges, you want to drag others down with you. Some hope! I've had this lot!"

Off he went, treading the white, untouched snow with such weight that his tracks at once blackened as they filled with water, snow melted by the force of his feet.

"Bektai, listen to me." Tanabai caught him up. "I'll explain everything."

"Explain to someone else—find some other fools to listen to you."

"Stop, Bektai. Let's talk it over."

Bektai walked on, not wishing to listen.

"You'll end up in court!"

"Better to be in court on trial, than to live like that!" Bektai growled back and didn't look round.

"You're a deserter!"

Bektai walked on.

"They shot people like you at the front!"

Bektai walked on.

"Stop, I say." Tanabai seized him by the sleeve. But Bektai snatched his arm away and walked on.

"I won't let you, you've no right!"

Tanabai seized him by the shoulder and turned him round. But suddenly the white snow drifts whirled in his eyes and faded in smoke. The unexpected blow under the chin had swept him off his feet.

When he raised his swimming head, Bektai had already disappeared round the hill.

After him lay a trail of dark footmarks.

"The boy has let himself in for it," groaned Tanabai, getting up on to all fours. He got up. His hands were covered in filth and snow.

He got his breath back, rounded up Bektai's flock and, downcast, drove them to his own fold.

17

Two riders left the village and set off into the mountains. One was on a dun horse and the other on a bay. The tails of their horses were tied in tight knots—they had a long ride before them. Dirt, mixed with snow, spattered and flew from under the hooves in splashes and lumps.

Gul'sary went on a tight rein at a firm, energetic pace. The pacer had not been ridden while his master had been in bed at home. His master was not riding him now, but some unknown man in a leather coat and with a thick raincoat open on top. His clothes had a smell of paint and rubber. Choro rode behind on the other horse. This was because he had lent the pacer to his comrade from region. But it was all the same to Gul'sary who rode on his back. Since they had taken him from the herd, from his old master, many different people had ridden him, kind and unkind, easy and difficult in the saddle. He had fallen into the hands of wild men, too. They were dreadful on a horse. Such a man would push him hard and then suddenly draw in on the reins, make him rear up and then again press him on and again draw up to a dead stop. The man had no idea what he was doing, his only concern was that all should see who was riding on the pacer. Gul'sary was already used to anything. The only thing that he asked was not to be left standing bored in the stable. He still had that one passion, to run, run and run again. It made no difference which man he carried. But it did make a difference to the riders on which horse they rode. They had been given the dun pacer and that meant that they were respected and feared. Gul'sary was strong and beautiful. His rider had a sure, steady mount.

This time the rider was the regional procurator, Segizbaev, sent down with full powers to the *kolkhoz*. He was accompanied by the *partorg* of the *kolkhoz*, who also commanded respect. The *partorg* did not speak; no doubt he was worried that all was not well up at the lambing. Very bad in fact. Let him be silent! Let him be frightened! This was no time to start empty chatter; the lower orders had to be cautious in front of their superiors, otherwise there would be no order at all. Some people behave simply with their subordinates, then they receive such a blow from them that dust flies out of them as from an old coat. Power—it's a big affair, it's responsibility; not everyone can measure up to it.

Segizbaev rode with such thoughts, rising and falling in the saddle in time with the pacer's movement. One could not say that he was in a bad mood, although he was on his way to investigate the shepherds and knew that he would find little there to gladden his heart. Winter and spring were in collision, neither would give ground and in this collision the sheep suffered most—the young ones died, the wearied ewes died and nothing could be done for them. It happened every year. Everyone knew it for a fact. But as they had sent him with full powers, he just had to find a scapegoat. Somewhere in the dark depths of his heart he knew that the high percentage of losses in the region was to his advantage. In the final analysis, he, the regional procurator, and just a member of the bureau of the regional council, could not be held responsible for the situation with the stock rearing. It was the first secretary who was responsible. He's new, not been long in the region, let him be answerable. But he, Segizbaev, would see. Let them, up there, look out as well, perhaps they had made a mistake when they appointed someone from outside. Segizbaev had been disappointed when it had happened and could not get used to the idea that they had passed him over. He had been procurator here for a long time and had often shown his mettle. Never mind, he had his friends who would support him. It was well overdue for him to go over to party work; he had got stuck as a procurator. The pacer was a good horse, he moved like a ship, undeterred by dirt or mire. The *partorg*'s horse was already in a lather, while his was just a bit damp.

Choro also was thinking. He looked very ill. A yellow tinge had spread over his thin face; his eyes were sunken. He had suffered with his heart trouble for so long, and the longer it went on, the worse it got. His heart was heavy. Yes, Tanabai was right; the president shouted, made a lot of noise and achieved absolutely nothing. He spent most of his time at the regional centre, he always seemed to have some business there. They were to have raised the matter at a party meeting, but at region they said that the matter should wait. What was there to wait for? People said that Aldanov himself wanted to go; perhaps that was why. It would be better if he did. It was also time for Choro to go. What use was he? He was always ill. His son, Samansur, had come on holiday and had also advised him to retire. Of course he could give up the work, but was it his conscience? Samansur was not a silly boy and understood many things better than his father. He was always talking about how things should be run on the farms. He was, no doubt, being taught sound stuff; with time, no doubt things would turn out like the professors taught, but in the meantime there's a trial or an investigation; his father would no doubt keep on to the end. But he could never get away from his grief anywhere. You cannot just run away and hide yourself. What would people say? He had promised, encouraged, got the *kolkhoz* into inextricable debt and was he now to rest? No, he would have no rest, there would be none, it was better to stand fast to the end. They would help, it could not be delayed so long. If only it would come more quickly. Real help too, not like this one here beside him. "We will have them on trial," he had said, "for the disorganization." Well, go ahead and have your trial. You cannot cure a situation like this with a gaol sentence. He's riding along there, all frowns, as if those up there in the mountains are simple criminals and that he, on his own, is fighting to defend the *kolkhoz*. Indeed he could spit on it all. He's just putting on airs. But try and tell him that!

18

The great mountains were covered with grey haze. Forgotten by the sun, they stretched up grimly like offended giants. Spring was not on its best form but damp and dull.

Tanabai was in trouble in his shed. It was cold, yet airless. Several ewes had lambed at once and there was no place to put the young ones. You could shout as much as you liked. Pandemonium, bleating and pushing animals. All wanted to eat, all wanted to drink and they were all dying off like flies. Now his wife was in bed with her bad back. She wanted to get up but was still very stiff. What would be, would be. He had no strength left.

Bektai would not leave his thoughts and a useless fury stifled Tanabai. Not because he had left him—he was free to do that—and not because he had deserted his flock like a cuckoo her eggs in another bird's nest. In the end they would send someone to take on his sheep; but his fury was because he had been unable to reply to Bektai, so that his skin peeled for shame, so that the earth held no joy for him! Little boy! Sniveller! But Tanabai himself, an old communist who had given his whole life to the *kolkhoz*, could not find those words to give him his due answer. Bektai had flung away his shepherd's crook and walked off, the puppy! Had Tanabai really thought that that would happen? When had he imagined that people would mock at his work, so dear to him?

"Enough!" He stopped the train of thought, but a minute later it started up again.

Another ewe had produced twins, fine little fellows ... But could they survive? The sheep's udder was empty and where else would milk come from. It meant that they too would die. What a disaster!

There they lay already dead and stiff. Tanabai collected the corpses and was carrying them out when his daughter ran up, out of breath.

144

"Father, some important-looking people are coming."

"Let them come," growled Tanabai, "you go back and look after your mother."

As he went out of the shed, Tanabai saw two riders. "Ah, Gul'sary!" He was glad. It struck the old chord in his heart. "We haven't seen one another for a long time! Look how he moves, still the same old style." One of the men was Choro. But he could not recognise the other, in a leather coat, who was riding the pacer. Someone from region, no doubt.

"Well, come along. At last," he thought maliciously. At least he could now complain, cry over his duty . . . no, he would not whine, let them do the blushing. Was it possible? They had left him to get on with it, cope with the disaster and now they were appearing . . .

Tanabai did not wait around for them to arrive; he went behind the shed and threw the dead lambs on the pile. He did not hurry himself.

Now they had arrived, the horses panting. Choro looked miserable, with a guilty expression. He knew that he would have to answer his friend. But that fellow on the pacer was angry, threatening and did not even greet Tanabai. Instead he opened up at once.

"What a disgrace! Everywhere it's the same! Look what is happening!" He was enraged as he spoke to Choro. Then he turned on Tanabai.

"What's all this? What are you doing, comrade?" He nodded in the direction where Tanabai had carried out the dead lambs. "You're a shepherd and a communist and your lambs are dying."

"They probably don't know that I'm a communist," said Tanabai caustically. Suddenly it seemed as if a spring had broken inside and all at once his heart was empty, indifferent and bitter.

"What's that?" Segizbaev went purple, lost his tongue for a moment and then, finding it again, "You made socialist promises?" He jerked at the head of the pacer as if in warning.

"I made them."

"What did you say then?"

"I don't remember."

"That's the reason why your lambs are dying!" Again Segizbaev pointed with his whip handle in the direction of the shed and rose up in his stirrups, inspired with the chance of teaching this insolent shepherd a lesson. But his first attack fell on Choro.

"What sort of control is this? People don't even know what they promised! They wreck the plan, they destroy the animals! What sort of job are you doing here? How do you educate your communists? What sort of communist is this one, I ask you!"

Choro made no answer, he hung his head and fiddled with his reins.

"A sort of one," Tanabai answered quietly for Choro.

"A fine sort of one. Yes, you're a wrecker! You destroy communal property! You're an enemy of the people! Your place is in gaol, not in the party! You have made a mockery of the socialist competition!"

"Yes—my place is in gaol, in gaol." Tanabai agreed quietly. But his lips were moving, laughing from a heart-rending onset of maddened rage bursting from resentment and bitterness, from all that had overfilled his cup of patience.

"Now," he flung the words at Segizbaev, "What more have you to say to me?"

"Why are you talking like this, Tanabai?" Choro broke in. "Why? Explain everything in a reasonable way."

"So that's it! I've got to explain. Why did you come then, Choro?" Tanabai shouted. "Why did you come? I'm asking you. To tell me my lambs are dying? I know that myself! To tell me I'm sitting in it right up to my neck? I know that too! That I've been a fool to flatter people all my life for the sake of the *kolkhoz*? Yes, and I know that too!"

"Tanabai! Tanabai! Think what you're saying!" Choro leaped from his saddle, white as a sheet.

"Keep away!" Tanabai pushed him aside. "I've spat on my promises, I've spat on my whole life! Get away from me! My place is in gaol! Why did you bring along this new overlord, this *manap* in the leather coat? So that he could mock me? So that he could put me in gaol? Come on then, you swine, put me in gaol!"

Tanabai turned to take hold of something and his hands fell

146

on the pitchfork resting against the wall. He advanced, brandish-
ing it, towards Segizbaev. "Now clear off, swine, clear off!"
Quite beside himself he waved the fork in front of him.

The terrified Segizbaev tried ineffectively to pull the pacer
first this way, then the other, but the fork beat the petrified horse
about the head, rose again, ringing, and again fell on his head. In
his rage Tanabai did not realise why Gul'sary's head was so feverishly pulling about, why the bridle was tearing at his red,
warm mouth and why the staring eyes of the horse so per-
plexedly and terribly flashed in front of him.

"Go away, Gul'sary! Out of my way! Let me get at this overlord in his leather!" yelled Tanabai, striking blow after blow on
the innocent head of the pacer.

The young *sakmanshchitsa,* who had hurried up, dragged at
his arm trying to snatch away the fork, but he flung her down.
Choro meanwhile had managed to remount.

"Get back! Let's get away! He'll kill us!" Choro moved in
towards Segizbaev, trying to shield him from Tanabai's on-
slaught.

Tanabai brandished the fork at him, but both riders made off
spurring on their horses. The dog raced after them, snapped at
the stirrups and the horses' tails.

Tanabai ran after them, tripping and picking up clods on the
run and flung them after the riders, shouting all the time.

"I should be in gaol! In gaol! Get off! Get away! I should be
in gaol! In gaol!"

Then he turned back, still mumbling and puffing.

"My place is in gaol, in gaol!" Running beside him, well
satisfied with his performance, was the dog. He expected the
praise due to him but his master paid no heed to him. The pale,
terrified Dzhaidar, supporting herself on a stick, stumbled out to
meet him.

"What have you done? What have you done?"

"All to no purpose."

"What do you mean, all to no purpose? Of course to no purpose!"

"I beat the pacer to no purpose."

"Are you mad? You know what you've done?"

"I know. I'm a wrecker. I'm an enemy of the people," he said, struggling for breath, then he became quiet, and covering his face with his hands, bending his head, wept loudly.

"Calm yourself, calm down," begged his wife, crying as well, but he wept on and on, rocking from side to side. Never before had Dzhaidar seen Tanabai in tears . . .

19

The meeting of the party bureau of the regional committee (*rai-kom*) was held on the third day after this extraordinary incident.

Tanabai Bakasov sat in the waiting room and waited for them to call him into the room in which they were discussing his case. He had thought a lot about the matter in the days between, but could not make up his mind whether he was to blame or not. He realised that he had committed a crime in raising his hand against a representative of the government, but if it had only been that, everything would have been quite simple. For his disgraceful behaviour, he was ready to take any punishment coming to him. But had he not, in giving way to a burst of anger, thrown all his concern for the *kolkhoz* to the winds, discredited all his worries and concern? Who would now believe him? Who would now understand him? "But perhaps they may yet understand?" He suddenly felt a new hope. "I will tell them everything; about this winter, the shed and the *yurta,* the lack of fodder, my nights without sleep, and about Bektai ... Let them consider these things. Can one run things like that?" He was no longer sorry that things had happened in the way they had. "Let them punish me," he thought, "Then, maybe, it will be easier for the others. Perhaps, after this they will take a good look at the shepherds' lot, at our living conditions, at our troubles." But a minute later, as he once more remembered all that he had been through, he became hard-hearted again and gripping his fists between his knees, said to himself with emphasis, "No, I'm not to blame at all, no!" Again he began to doubt ...

For some reason Ibraim was also sitting there in the waiting room. "What does he want here? He's come down like a vulture after carrion." Tanabai angrily turned away from him. But the other did not say a word and sighed as he looked at the bowed head of the shepherd.

"What are they taking so long about?" Tanabai shifted in his chair. "What more do they want? They've only to hit me." Behind the doors everyone should have arrived. The last to come, just a few minutes ago, had been Choro. Tanabai had recognised him by the horsehairs sticking to the calves of his boots. It was the yellowish hair of the dun pacer. "He must have been in a hurry, Gul'sary had got into a lather," he thought, but did not raise his head. The boots, with the streaks of horse's sweat and the hairs on the calves, made some undecided steps towards Tanabai, but then disappeared behind the doors. A long time dragged past before the secretary looked out of the door.

"Come in, comrade Bakasov."

Tanabai shuddered, got up, deafened by the thumping of his heart and with this unceasing cannonade in his ears went in to the room. His sight was clouded. He could scarcely make out the faces of the people sitting there.

"Sit down," the first secretary of the *raikom*, Kashkataev, motioned Tanabai to a chair at the end of the long table.

Tanabai sat down. He put his heavy hands on his knees and waited until the mistiness cleared from his eyes. Then he looked down the table. On the right hand of the first secretary sat Segizbaev with a haughty expression. Tanabai was so overcome with hate towards him that the mistiness at once fell away. The faces of all those at the table became clear and distinct. The darkest amongst them, deep purple, was the face of Segizbaev and the palest, entirely drained of blood, was that of Choro. He sat at the end, the nearest to Tanabai. His thin hands trembled nervously on the green baize of the table. The president of the *kolkhoz*, Aldanov, sitting opposite Choro, noisily sniffed as he looked around and frowned. He was not hiding his feelings about the matter before them. The others were still waiting. At last the first secretary looked up from the papers, which he had been studying in the file.

"We will now take the personal case of communist Bakasov," he said, firmly stressing each word.

"So-called communist," someone said with a spiteful snigger.

"They're malicious," thought Tanabai. "I can expect no

mercy from this lot. But why should I look for mercy? Am I a criminal?"

He was not to know that in the consideration of his case, two sides, in secret rivalry, would clash, each ready to make use of this deplorable incident for their own ends. One side, represented by Segizbaev and his allies, wished to try the strength of the new secretary, to try to get control of him. The other side, represented by Kashkataev himself, who had guessed that Segizbaev was after his job, was trying to think how to act so as not to get into difficulties and not to worsen relations with these dangerous people.

The *raikom* secretary read out the report of Segizbaev. In this were set down in detail all the offences committed in deed and word by Tanabai Bakasov, a shepherd of the *Belye Kamny* (White Stones) *kolkhoz*. There was nothing in the report which Tanabai could deny, but its tone, the form in which the charges were made against him, drove him to despair. He was covered in sweat from the realisation of his complete powerlessness against this monstrous paper. The report made by Segizbaev was more terrifying than the man himself. You could not fight against that with a pitchfork. All that Tanabai had planned to say in his defence fell down at once and lost its meaning in his own eyes, and turned into the wretched complaint of a shepherd at his normal difficulties. Was he not stupid? What was the value of his excuses before this dreadful paper? With whom had he thought he was fighting?

"Comrade Bakasov, do you agree with the correctness of the facts contained in the written statement by member of the bureau, comrade Segizbaev?" asked Kashkataev, when he had read the report.

Everyone was silent. It seemed as if everyone was struck with fear by this paper. The satisfied Aldanov looked round those at the table with a challenging expression, "You see now what goes on."

"Comrades, members of the bureau, perhaps you will allow me to explain some points in more detail." Segizbaev started off with a determined air. "I wish to anticipate straightaway some comrades who may attempt to describe the action of comrade Bakasov as a simple act of hooliganism. If it had been only that, then believe me, I would not have raised this matter in the bureau; we have other methods of dealing with hooligans. Nor is this a matter of an insult to my personal feelings. Behind me stands the bureau of the regional committee of the party; behind me stands, if you like, the whole party. I cannot allow vulgar abuse to be directed against its authority. But the main point is that this draws attention to the neglect in our political and educational work among communists and non-party people, it shows up serious shortcomings in the ideological work of the *raikom*. We are all responsible for the type of thoughts expressed by such rank-and-file communists as Bakasov. We have still to find out if he is the only one like this, or whether there are others who think like him. Take his expression, 'A new *manap* in a leather coat!' Let's leave the coat out of it. But according to Bakasov it seems that I, a Soviet man, a party plenipotentiary, am a new overlord, a fine gentleman, a *barin*, an oppressor of the people. Now you see! You understand what is hidden behind these words? I think no further comment is needed. Now another aspect. Despondent at the awful situation of the stock breeding in White Stones, in answer to the disgraceful words spoken by Bakasov, who had apparently forgotten his socialist duties and promises, I called him a wrecker, an enemy of the people and said that his place was not in the party, but in gaol. I realised that I had insulted him and I was ready to apologise to him. But now I am convinced that what I said is correct. I will not retract my words, and I confirm my view that Bakasov is a dangerous person with hostile intent ..."

After all that Tanabai had lived through in his life—the war from start to finish—he would not have believed that his heart could cry out with such a cry as it did now. With this cry, stifling the unceasing noise in his ears, his heart fell, rose, staggered, fell away again and tried to rise, but the bullets had struck home at point-blank range.

"Oh God," thought Tanabai, "where has everything gone, all that gave purpose to my life, the reason for my work? What have I achieved—I have become an enemy of the people. I have suffered because of a shed, wretched dung-bespattered lambs, because of the dissolute Bektai. What good does this do anybody."

"I will repeat once more the conclusions of my written

evidence," Segizbaev continued, weighing his words in their cast-iron order. "Bakasov hates our way of life; he hates the *kolkhoz*; he hates the socialist competition, he spits on all of this, he hates this whole life of ours. This he stated entirely openly in the presence of the *partorg* of the *kolkhoz*, comrade Sayakov. In his actions he displayed the basic elements of a criminal act, an attempt against a representative of the government in the execution of his duties. Please understand me, I am asking for Bakasov to be brought to trial and that as he leaves here he be taken into custody. His crime is fully within the terms of section 58. As for Bakasov remaining in the ranks of the party, there can be no question of that . . ."

Segizbaev knew that he had asked for too much, but he had calculated that even if the bureau did not consider it necessary to declare Tanabai Bakasov responsible under the law, at least his expulsion from the party was a foregone conclusion. Kashkataev just had to support this latter requirement and his, Segisbaev's position was the more secure.

"Tanabai Bakasov, what do you have to say about your action?" asked Kashkataev, already very irritated.

"Nothing. Everything has already been said," answered Tanabai. "It seems I was and remain a wrecker, an enemy of the people. Why do you need to know what I think? Judge for yourselves, you know best . . ."

"But do you consider yourself an honest communist?"

"I could not prove that now."

"Do you admit your guilt?"

"No."

"What, do you think you are wiser than everyone else?"

'No, on the contrary, more stupid than all the others."

"Please allow me to speak." A young man wearing a *komsomol* badge rose from his seat. He was younger than the others, undersized, thin-faced and looked quite a boy still.

Tanabai had only just noticed him. "Go on, boy, show no mercy," he said to himself. "Once upon a time I was the same as you, I had no pity."

Like a flash of lightning in far-away clouds, he saw that spot in the wheat field, by the track, where Kulubai had torn out and trampled the young plants. He saw everything quite clearly in his mind's eye and he shook with a silent cry in his heart.

The voice of Kashkataev brought him back to the present.

"Go ahead, Kerimbekov."

"I do not condone the act of comrade Bakasov. I think that he should receive the appropriate party reprimand. But I am not in agreement with comrade Segizbaev." There was a hint of uncertainty in Kerimbekov's voice. "At least I think that the case of Segizbaev himself ought to be raised."

"Well, what about that?" someone interrupted, "Is this the sort of standard you set yourselves in the *komsomol*?"

"Standards are the same everywhere," answered Kerimbekov, getting more nervous and blushing. He hesitated, choosing his words, and overcoming his restraint suddenly, as if in despair, began to speak bitingly and angrily.

"What right had you to insult a member of the *kolkhoz*, a shepherd and an old communist? You just try calling me an enemy of the people . . . your excuse is that you were depressed at the state of the stock breeding in the *kolkhoz*, but didn't it occur to you that this shepherd was no less upset than you? When you arrived did you concern yourself with his living conditions? How things were with him? Why the young animals were dying? No, and judging by your own report, you began to blame him immediately. It's no secret to anyone that the lambing season in the *kolkhozes* is a difficult time. I am often out there and I feel ashamed and uneasy in front of the *komsomol* shepherds, because we demand a lot from them and give them no real help. Have you seen what sort of lambing sheds there are on the *kolkhoz*, what the fodder situation is like? I am the son of a shepherd and I know how it is when the lambs die off. In the institute they taught us one thing and out on the farms things are still done in the old way. It makes your heart ache to see it . . ."

"Comrade Kerimbekov," Segizbaev broke in, "don't try to arouse our pity; feelings are a loose concept. Facts, facts are necessary, not feelings."

"Excuse me, but here we are not trying a criminal, we are looking at the case of a fellow communist, a party member," continued Kerimbekov. "The fate of a communist is being decided. So let us consider fully why comrade Bakasov acted as he did. His action must, of course, be judged, but how did it happen that one of the best herdsmen on the *kolkhoz*, namely Bakasov, got into such a position?"

"Sit down." Kashkataev was most displeased. "You are diverting us from the main issue, comrade Kerimbekov. It is absolutely clear to everyone here, in my opinion, that comrade Bakasov committed a most serious crime. What use is this? Who's heard of such a thing? We don't allow anyone to attack our plenipotentiaries with pitchforks, we do not allow anyone to challenge the authority of our workers. You should, comrade Kerimbekov, employ your time better in considering how to get *komsomol* affairs in order, rather than start up a discussion about hearts and feelings. Feelings are feelings and hard facts are hard facts. What Bakasov allowed himself to do should be a warning to us and of course, he should not remain in the party. Comrade Sayakov, do you as *partorg*, confirm all this evidence?" He turned to Choro.

"Yes, I confirm it," started the pale Choro, slowly getting to his feet, "But I want to explain . . ."

"To explain what?"

"Firstly, I would request that we consider the case of Bakasov in the local party organisation."

"That's not necessary. You will be able to inform your party organisation and members later on about the decision of the *raikom* bureau. Do you wish to say anything else?"

"I wished to explain . . ."

"What is there to explain, comrade Sayakov? The anti-party behaviour of Bakasov is clear for all to see. There's nothing to explain. And you yourself carry some responsibility. We will punish you for the failure to educate this communist. Why did you try to persuade comrade Segizbaev not to put this matter before the bureau? Did you wish to keep it covered up? Disgraceful! Sit down."

The arguments started. The director of the machine and tractor repair station and the editor of the regional newspaper supported Kerimbekov. For a moment it even seemed that they would succeed in upholding Tanabai's cause. But he, crushed and down, was not listening to anyone. He just asked himself, "What has happened to everything on which I based my life? It's quite clear that no one here is worried about the state of affairs in the flocks, in the herds. What a fool I was. I have used up my life for the sake of the *kolkhoz*, for the sake of the sheep and lambs. Now none of this is taken into consideration. Now I'm a dangerous element. Well, the devil take you. Do what you like with me; if things get better because of that, then I won't be sorry. Throw me out on my neck. There's only one thing left for me, cut me out, have no pity!"

The president of the *kolkhoz*, Aldanov, rose to speak. By his expression and gestures Tanabai saw that he was defaming someone, but whom exactly was not clear to him until he heard the words ". . . fetter . . . the pacer, Gul'sary."

"What do you think?" Aldanov was most upset. "He even threatened to brain me, simply because we had to put fetters on the horse's legs. Comrade Kashkataev, comrade members of the bureau. I ask you, as president of the *kolkhoz*, to rid us of this Bakasov. His place is indeed in gaol. He hates all those in authority. Comrade Kashkataev, outside that door are witnesses who can confirm the threats made against me by Bakasov. Can we have them in?"

"No, there is no need for that." Kashkataev screwed up his face in disgust. "We have heard enough, sit down."

Then the voting began.

"There is one proposal—to expel comrade Bakasov from the party. Who is in favour of this?"

"One moment, comrade Kashkataev," once again Kerimbekov was on his feet.

"Comrades, members of the bureau, are we not making a serious mistake? There is an alternative proposal—to confine the matter to a severe reprimand and to make an entry in the personal record of Bakasov and at the same time to reprimand a member of the bureau, Segizbaev, for the insult to the party and to the personal honour of comrade Bakasov, for the unacceptable methods used by Segizbaev, when acting as the plenipotentiary of the *raikom*."

"Demagogy!" roared Segizbaev.

"Calm down, comrades!" said Kashkataev. "You are at a sitting of the *raikom* bureau and not in your own homes; please observe some discipline."

Now everything depended on him, as the first secretary of the *raikom*. He dealt with the matter just as Segizbaev had expected.

"I do not consider it necessary to pronounce Bakasov as criminally responsible," he said, "but there is no place for him in the ranks of the party; comrade Segizbaev is quite right on this point. We will vote. Who is for the expulsion of Bakasov?"

There were seven members in the bureau. Three voted for expulsion, three against. Kashkataev had the casting vote. After a moment's thought, he raised his hand in favour of the resolution. Tanabai did not even see this. He only knew the result when he heard Kashkataev say to the secretary, "Write down in the record, 'by a decision of the *raikom* bureau, comrade Bakasov is expelled from membership of the party'."

"That's all," Tanabai said to himself, his feelings deadened.

"But I ask for a vote on a reprimand for Segizbaev." Kerimbekov would not give up the fight.

It would have been possible not to put this to the vote, to reject it, but Kashkataev decided that a vote should be taken. There was a secret reason for this.

"Who votes for the proposition of comrade Kerimbekov? Please raise your hand!" Again three votes to three; again Kashkataev lifted his hand and thus saved Segizbaev from the reprimand.

"But will he understand and appreciate what I have done? Who knows? He is crafty and cunning."

The people began to shuffle around in their chairs as if preparing to leave. Tanabai decided that all was over, stood up and silently, looking at no one, made for the door.

"Bakasov, where are you off to?" Kashkataev stopped him, "You will have to leave your party card."

"Leave it?" Only now did Tanabai realise the full import of what had just been happening.

"Yes. Put it on the table. You are no longer a member of the party and no longer have the right to carry it."

Tanabai began to search for the card. He took his time in the silence. It was there, deep down, under his pullover, under his jacket, in a leather purse made by Dzhaidar. Tanabai carried this purse on a strap across his shoulder. At last he got it out and extracted the card. He put it, warm from his chest and smelling of him, on the cold polished table before Kashkataev. He shivered, for he felt cold. Again looking at no one, he stuffed the purse under his coat and began to leave.

"Comrade Bakasov," he heard behind him, from the table, the sympathetic voice of Kerimbekov. "What have you to say for yourself in your defence? You have said nothing here. Perhaps it was difficult for you to do so? We hope that the doors are not closed for you and that sooner or later you will be able to return to the party. Go on, say what you are thinking now."

Painfully and with difficulty Tanabai turned round at the request of this unknown youth who was still trying to lessen his grief.

"What can I say," he said sadly, "you cannot convince all these people here. I'll just say that I am not guilty, even though I did raise my hand in anger, even if I did say things that I should not have said. I cannot explain this to you. That's all, I think."

An oppressive silence followed.

"Hmm. So you feel resentful against the party," said Kashkataev with a note of irritation. "Well, well, comrade. The party is putting you back on the right lines, and has saved you from a trial in the courts, but you are still not satisfied and feel angry! Indeed you are not worthy of the title of party member. How indeed could the doors remain open for you."

Tanabai left the committee building outwardly calm. He was too calm and this was bad. It was a warm, sunny day, towards evening. People outside were going about their business, the children were playing in the square by the club. Tanabai felt sick looking at all this as he thought about what had happened to him. He wanted to get home as quickly as possible, back to the mountains, back home. Before something else unpleasant happened to him.

Standing beside his horse at the tethering point was Gul'sary. The big, strong, long horse, shifted from foot to foot as Tanabai approached and looked at his old master with quiet, trusting, warm eyes. The pacer had already forgotten that Tanabai had struck him with the pitchfork, for he was a horse . . .

"Forget and forgive, Gul'sary," whispered Tanabai to the pacer. "I'm in real trouble, very real trouble," he sobbed with his arms around the horse's neck. But he controlled himself and did not give way to shameful tears in front of passers-by. He mounted his own horse and made off towards home.

Choro caught him up past the Aleksandrovka rise. As soon as he heard the pacer's hooves behind him, Tanabai angrily pressed his lips together and bent over his saddle. He did not look round. His resentment darkened his soul and darkened his eyes. This Choro of today was not the one whom he had known before. Today Kashkataev had only to raise his voice and Choro had sat down at once like a small schoolboy. What more was there to say? People trust him but he is afraid to tell the truth. He protects himself and chooses his words carefully. Who has taught him this? Tanabai may be a simple worker, but Choro is literate, knows everything and has spent his life in a position of responsibility. Surely he can see that things are not as the Segizbaevs and Kashkataevs say that they are; their words sound all right on the surface, but inside they are empty lies. Who is deceiving whom and why?

Tanabai did not turn his head even when Choro had drawn level and was riding beside him, holding the high-spirited pacer in check.

"I thought, Tanabai, that we would be leaving together," he said, getting his breath back, "I hurried up but you had already gone on."

"What's it to you?" answered Tanabai, not looking at him. "You go your own way."

"Let's talk it over. Don't look away, Tanabai. Let's talk as friends, as communists," began Choro and stopped short.

"I'm not your friend and still less a communist! You yourself have not been a communist for a long time. You just pretend to be one . . ."

"Do you really mean that?" asked Choro in a hushed voice.

"Of course I mean it. I have not yet learnt to pick my words. I don't know what, when or how to speak. Good-bye. You go straight on and I turn off here." Tanabai turned his horse off the road and still not looking back at his friend, made off across the fields towards the mountains.

He did not see Choro turn deathly pale, how he wanted to stop him, stretched out his hand after him writhing in pain, clutched at his chest and then fell across the pacer's mane, gasping for breath.

"I'm ill," whispered Choro, in agony from the pain in his heart. "Oh, how bad it is this time," he groaned, turning blue and still gasping. "Quickly, quickly, take me home, Gul'sary, home."

The pacer carried him back to the village, over the dark, empty steppe. The man's voice had frightened the pacer who had heard in its tones something strange and terrible. Gul'sary flattened his ears and neighed as he ran. The man in his saddle suffered meanwhile, writhing and feverishly holding on to the mane with hands and teeth. The reins swung, dangling loose from Gul'sary's neck as he raced homewards.

20

At a late hour, while Tanabai was still on his way up to the mountains, a rider was dashing down the streets of the village, making the dogs bark.

"Oi! Who's at home, come out!" he called to the occupants of the houses. "Come to the office to a special party meeting."

"What's happened? What's the hurry?"

"I don't know," answered the rider, "But Choro is asking for us all to come as quickly as possible!"

Meanwhile Choro himself was sitting in the office. He had slumped over the table, resting on one shoulder, bent and gasping, pressing his chest with his whole hand under his shirt. He groaned from pain and bit his lips. A cold sweat broke out on his now greenish face, his eyes were like dark holes deep in their sockets. At times he was delirious and once more it seemed to him that the pacer was still carrying him over the dark steppe. He wanted to call to Tanabai but he, having flung those harsh, burning words in farewell, would not look round. The words of Tanabai burnt deep into his heart, into his soul . . .

They had carried the *partorg* here from the stable, after he had rested a short while on the hay. The stable lads had wanted to take him straight home, but he would not hear of it. They had sent someone round to collect the communists together and they expected them to arrive at any moment.

The caretaker had lit the lamp and then left Choro on his own. Now she was busy with the stove in the front room but every now and again she looked in through the half-opened door and shook her head.

Choro was waiting with time dripping away. Only now, as the span of life given to him at birth was dripping every second away in bitter, hard drops, did he realise the price he had paid for that long life. He had not had time to realise how his days and years were passing by in work and worry. Not everything he had touched in his life had been as successful as he would have wished. He had striven and fought, sometimes he had retreated to get round corners so that life would not be so hard. But he had not avoided trouble. He had tried before to avoid clashing head-long with the force which was now pinning him to the wall, but now he had reached the end and there was no way out. If only he had thought earlier, if only he had faced facts earlier . . .

Time was still dripping away in bitter, hollow-sounding drops. "How long everyone is taking to come, how long I have to wait!"

"If only I can hold on," Choro thought in his fear. "If only I can succeed in saying everything there is to be said!" He held on to his ebbing life with a soundless, despairing cry. He was gathering up his strength for the last and final battle. "I will tell them everything, what was discussed, how the bureau meeting went and how they expelled Tanabai from the party. I will let them know that I disagree with the *raikom* decision; let them know that I disagree with the expulsion of Tanabai. I will say everything I think about Aldanov. Let them listen to him later on, after I have had my word. Let the communists decide! I will tell them all about myself, what sort of a person I am. I will talk about our *kolkhoz*, about people . . . if only I can last out, if only they will come quickly, quickly . . ."

His wife arrived first with his medicine. She was terrified, exclaiming, complaining and crying, "Are you in your right mind? Haven't you had enough of these meetings? Let's go home! Look at yourself! My God, at least think about yourself!"

Choro did not wish to listen. He waved her away, but drank his medicine. His teeth rattled on the glass and drops fell on his chest.

"No need to worry, I'm better already," he said, trying to breathe more evenly. "Wait there at home, take me back later. Don't be frightened, off you go."

When he heard the steps of the people arriving along the street, Choro sat up straight, overcame his pain, gathered all his strength in order to fulfil what he considered his final act of duty.

"What's happened? How are you, Choro?" they asked.

"I'm all right. I will tell you everything now, as soon as everyone gets here," he answered.

Time passed by with bitter, hollow-sounding drops.

When all the communists had arrived, Choro Sayakov got to his feet, took off his hat and declared the party meeting open . . .

21

Tanabai returned home when it was already night. Dzhaidar came out with a torch. She waited and looked at him, looked through him into his heart.

From her first glance she understood the misfortune that had hit her husband. He silently unharnessed the horse and took off the saddle while she held the lamp for him; he said nothing. "If only he had got drunk at region, perhaps it would have made it easier for him," she thought. But still he did not say a word and his silence was terrible. Intending to please him, she had wanted to tell him that a little fodder had been brought, some straw and barley flour, that it had got warmer, the lambs had gone out to pasture and were already eating a little grass.

"They've taken away Bektai's flock. They sent out a new shepherd for it," she said.

"I don't give a damn for them, for Bektai, or the flock or for your shepherd!"

"You're tired?"

"Why should I be tired? They've only expelled me from the party!"

"Not so loud, the *sakmanshchitsy* will hear."

"What do you mean, not so loud? What have I got to hide? They've thrown me out, like a dog and that's all there is to it. That's all I deserve. That's all you deserve too. It's enough for us, isn't it? What are you standing there for? What are you looking at?"

"Go and rest."

"I know what's best for me."

Tanabai went into the shed. He looked the sheep over. Then he went into the sheep-fold, and wandered around in the dark before returning to the shed. He couldn't settle down. He had refused to eat and he had refused to talk. He flung himself down on to the straw in the corner and lay motionless. His life, his worries, his cares had all lost their meaning. He did not want anything. He didn't want to live, he didn't want to think.

He twisted and turned, he wanted just to sleep, to forget, but in this state how could he escape from himself? Again he recalled how Bektai had walked away leaving dark tracks in the white snow, and how he had been unable to give him any answer. He recalled once more Segizbaev shouting as he sat on the pacer, pouring abuse on him, threatening to put him into gaol; then presenting Tanabai at the *raikom* bureau as a wrecker, an enemy of the people and at that point everything, all his life, had finished. Once again he longed to seize the pitchfork and rush shouting into the night, to bellow wildly at the whole world until he fell into the ravine and broke his neck.

As he dozed off he felt death would be better than life. Yes, yes, death was better . . .

He woke with a heavy head. For some moments he could not make out where he was or what had happened. Around him the sheep were baaing, the lambs were bleating. So he was in the shed. Dawn had already come up. Why had he woken up? Why? It would have been better not to wake up at all. The only thing left was to die, he should kill himself . . .

. . . Later on he was drinking water from the stream by the handful; cold, ice-cold water with a thin layer of crackling ice. The water flowed noisily between his shivering fingers as he cupped it up in his hands and sluiced it over his face. After resting, he had come to his senses and only then had understood the fully ridiculous nature of those thoughts of suicide, all the stupidity of a crime against oneself. How could anyone take their one and only life! Are the Segizbaevs of this world worth that? No. Tanabai will go on living, he will yet move mountains!

On his return home he hid the gun and the cartridges without being noticed and worked hard all day. He wanted to be more gentle with his wife, his daughters and with the *sakmanshchitsy,* but he was careful not to let the women suspect anything. They worked hard like on a normal day, as if nothing had happened. Tanabai was grateful for this and went on working without a word. He went out to the pasture and helped to drive the flock home.

In the evening the weather got worse; there was bound to be

rain or snow. The mountains were lost in cloud, which filled the sky. Again he had to think how to protect the young lambs from the cold. Again he had to clean out the shed and lay down straw so that the wave of death should not recur. Tanabai was gloomy, but he was trying to forget what happened and not to lose heart.

It was already getting dark when a rider arrived. Dzhaidar met him and they were talking about something while Tanabai was still working in the shed.

"Come out here a moment," his wife called, "there's someone to see you." As she called, he felt at once that something was wrong.

He came out. They exchanged greetings. It was the shepherd from the neighbouring land.

"What's brought you here, Aitbai. Get down from your horse. Where have you come from now?"

"From the village. I had dropped in there. They asked me to tell you that Choro is seriously ill and asked you to come."

"Not Choro again!" His anger flared up, he did not want to see him. "What for? Am I a doctor? He's always ill. I've enough trouble here—I'm up to my neck in work. The weather's getting worse, too."

"It's up to you, Tanake, whether to go or not, you're the best judge. But I've told you that they've asked for you. Good-bye. I must get along, it'll be night soon."

Aitbai rode off, but then stopped.

"Think it over all the same, Tanake. He's really bad. They've called his son home from his studies. They've gone to meet him at the station."

"Thank you for telling me. But I won't be going."

"He'll go." Dzhaidar was ashamed. "Don't worry, he'll go."

Tanabai did not say anything, but when Aitbai had gone, he turned angrily on his wife:

"You must give up this habit of answering for me. I know what to do for myself. If I've said I won't go, that means I won't go."

"Think what you're saying, Tanabai."

"I've nothing to think about. That's an end to it. I thought to such an extent that they expelled me from the party. I've no one.

166

If I fall ill, don't let anyone come to me. I'll die on my own." He waved his hand angrily and went back into the shed.

But in his heart there was no peace. He attended the lambing ewes, put the young ones in a corner, tried to silence the noisy sheep, pushed them, sent them to the devil and mumbled away.

"He should have retired long ago and not have suffered so with his health. All his life he kept falling ill, groaning, clasping at his heart, but wouldn't get out of the saddle. What a boss he was to me! I don't want to see him after this! He can take it as he likes, but I'm offended too; this is no one else's business . . ."

Outside it was now quite dark; a little snow was falling and the silence was such that you could even hear the snowflakes hitting the ground.

Tanabai did not go into the *yurta*; he was avoiding any talk with his wife and she was not coming to him. He thought: "Sit there and don't try to make me go. It's all the same to me now. Choro and I are now strangers to one another. He has his furrow, I have mine. We were once friends, but no more. If I am his friend, where was he earlier? No, it's all the same to me now . . ."

All the same Dzhaidar did come. She brought his coat, his new boots, sash, gloves and the hat which he wore for long rides.

"Get dressed," she said.

"You're wasting your time. I'm going nowhere."

"Don't waste time. Something could happen, which you will regret for the rest of your life."

"I won't regret anything. Nothing will happen to him. He'll get over it. It's not the first time."

"Tanabai, I've never asked anything from you before. But now I am; give me your resentment, give me your grief. Go! Be a man!"

"No, I won't go." Tanabai shook his head obstinately. "It means nothing to me now. You're only thinking about polite behaviour, about my 'duty', or what people will say. But I don't want to know any more about it."

"Think again, Tanabai—while I just go and see that nothing has fallen out of the fire on to the carpet."

She went, leaving his clothing there, but he did not move. He sat in the corner unable to restrain his feelings. He could not forget those words he had spoken to Choro. And now? "Good morning, I've come to see you; how are you getting on? Can I help in any way?" No, he couldn't do that, it was not his way.

Dzhaidar returned.

"You've not got dressed yet?"

"Don't go on, I've said I won't go."

"Get up." She spoke in a rage. To his own surprise he got up at her command, like a soldier. She came up to him and looked at him in the dim light of the lamp, with her sad, angry eyes.

"If you're not a man, if you've no human feelings, if you're a dribbling old woman, then I'll go in your place and you stay here to snivel! I'll go straightaway. Go and saddle my horse at once!"

In obedience to her he went to saddle the horse. Snow was falling. It was dark, and the darkness seemed to circle around noiselessly in a slow whirl, like water in a deep pool. It was too dark to see the outline of the mountains. "Here's another problem. Where will she get to in the middle of the night?" he thought, as he threw on the saddle in the dark. "There's no way of dissuading her. No, she will not give in. Threaten to kill her, she still wouldn't give in. But, supposing she strayed off the track? She'd only have herself to blame . . ."

Tanabai had saddled the horse and began to feel ashamed of himself.

"I'm a beast, nothing more. Resentment has made me quite simple. I've been showing off in front of her—look how unhappy I am, how shockingly bad everything is for me. I've exasperated her. What has she got to do with it? Why am I getting at her? I cannot do any good. I'm a useless person, yes, a beast and nothing else."

Tanabai wavered. It was not easy to go back on what he had said. He went back, his eyes down like a bull.

"Have you saddled up?"

"Yes."

"Well, get on your way." Dzhaidar handed him his coat.

Tanabai began to dress in silence. He was glad that his wife had made the first move towards peace, but, all the same he made a final show of bravado.

"Perhaps I'll just go in the morning?"

"No, you get going at once. It'll be too late otherwise."

The night in the mountains went round and round like a quiet backwater. The big flakes of the last spring snow fell smoothly and gently. Tanabai rode alone amid the dark hills to answer the call of his rejected friend. The snow lay on his head, shoulders, beard and hands. He sat motionless in the saddle, not shaking off the snow. He thought better like that. He was thinking about Choro, about all that had held them so close together for so many years, Choro teaching him to read and write, and joining the *komsomol* together and later the party. He remembered how they had worked on the construction of the canal together and how it had been Choro who had first brought him the copy of the paper with his photograph and a paragraph about him in it. Choro had been the first to congratulate him, the first to shake his hand.

Tanabai's hardened heart softened and then melted altogether; he was seized with an aching worry. "How is he? Perhaps he really is bad? Why have they sent for his son? Or is there something he wants to say? Or to discuss?"

It was already light as the snow was still coming down. Tanabai hurried his horse on at a trot. Once over those hills, below would be the village. How is Choro? Faster!

Suddenly in the quiet of the early morning, a distant and dim voice could be heard from the direction of the village. A shout broke off and died. Tanabai stopped his horse and listened but now heard nothing. Perhaps it had been his imagination.

The horse took Tanabai up the hill. Below him, amongst the white snow-covered orchards, amongst the bare gardens, lay the streets of the village, still empty at this time of the morning. No one was about. But by one house there was the black mass of a crowd and by the trees were tethered saddled horses. This was Choro's home. Why had so many people gathered there? Had something happened? Surely not . . .

Rising in his stirrups, Tanabai feverishly swallowed a big mouthful of freezing cold, frosty air; suddenly he spurred the horse down the road, "It can't be! How could it happen? It just can't be!" He felt sick at heart, as if he was to blame for what had, without doubt, just happened down there. Choro, his only friend, had asked him to come for one last meeting before they parted for ever and he had jibbed, obstinately nursed his resentment. What was he worth after this? Why had his wife not spat in his face? What could be more sacred than the last request of a dying man?

Again Tanabai saw before him that road over the steppe, along which Choro had ridden on the pacer to catch up with him. What had he said to him? Could he forgive himself for that?

As if delirious Tanabai rode along the snow-covered street, bent under the weight of guilt and shame, and suddenly he noticed by Choro's house a large group of horsemen. They approached in a silent mass, and suddenly as one they rocked in their saddles and gave forth the mourning cry.

"Oibai, baurymai! Oibaiai, baurym!"

"The Kazakhs have come," realised Tanabai and then knew that he had no more hopes to cling to. The Kazakh neighbours had come from over the river and were mourning for Choro as if he were their brother, for he was their close neighbour and known throughout the whole district. "Thank you, brothers," he thought, "from the old men and the fathers, in sorrow and grief together, at weddings and at races together. Now weep, weep together with us!"

Then after them he too gave a great straining, heart-rending cry over the waking village:

"Choro-o-o! Choro-o-o! Choro-o-o!"

As he trotted along, he hung first from the left side of the saddle, then from the right side, and wept for his friend who had gone from this world.

Here was the house; Gul'sary stood there by the house in a mourning horse-cloth. The snow was settling on him and melting. The pacer without his master had to stand there with an empty saddle.

Tanabai fell on to the mane of his horse, then rose up again. All around him, indistinguishable as if in a mist, were people's faces weeping. He did not hear when someone said:

"Lift Tanabai down from his saddle. Lead him to Choro's son."

Several pairs of hands took hold of him and helped him down and led him through the crowd.

"Forgive me, Choro, forgive!" wept Tanabai.

In the yard with his face to the wall stood Choro's son, the student, Samansur. He turned to Tanabai in tears, they embraced together and wept.

"Your father is no more; my Choro is no more! Forgive me, Choro, forgive!" Tanabai choked through his tears.

Then they parted them. And here Tanabai saw her beside him, amongst the women, Byubyuzhan. She looked at him and silently wept. Tanabai wept all the more.

He was weeping for everything, for all his losses, for Choro, for his sin against him, because he could not take back those words which he had flung at him on the road; he was weeping for the woman who was now standing beside him like a stranger, for that love, that stormy night, because she was left alone, because she had already grown old; he wept for his pacer, Gul'sary, standing out there in his mourning horse-cloth; he wept over all his insults and troubles, over everything which had not been wept over before.

"Forgive me, Choro, forgive!" he repeated. It was as if he was begging her forgiveness, too.

He longed for Byubyuzhan to come up and console him, to wipe away his tears, but she did not come. She stood there and wept.

Others consoled him, "Enough, Tanabai. You will not help with your tears! Calm yourself!"

He felt more bitter, more hurt.

22

They buried Choro that afternoon. The misty disc of the sun shone through the faded layers of motionless clouds. Soft white flakes of snow still hung in the air. The funeral procession dragged its way over the white fields like a black, silent stream. This stream seemed to have made its bed for the first time, having suddenly appeared. In front on a truck with the sides down lay the dead Choro. He was tightly wound in a white winding sheet. His wife, children and relatives sat by him. All the rest of the mourners followed on horseback. But two walked on foot behind the truck—the son, Samansur and Tanabai, who was leading the empty-saddled horse of his friend, the pacer Gul'sary.

The track outside the village lay through soft, level snow; it lay behind the procession, wide and dark and marked out by the horses' hooves. It was marking Choro's last journey, leading to the hill in the cemetery where it finished; there was no return for Choro.

As he led the pacer Tanabai said to himself, as if to the horse, "Here we are, Gul'sary. We have lost our Choro. He is no more, he has gone . . . Why did you not shout at me then? Why did you not stop me? But God did not give you the gift of speech. I am a man, but it seems that I am lower than you, a horse. I left my friend on the road, I did not look round, I did not think. I killed Choro, I killed him with my words . . ."

All the way up to the cemetery Tanabai was begging Choro for forgiveness. As he got down into the grave, together with Samansur, he said to Choro as he laid his body in its eternal resting place, "Forgive me, Choro. Farewell. Do you hear, Choro, forgive me!"

The earth fell into the grave first in little bits, then in whole streams as the spades began their work. It filled the grave and then grew up as a snowy hillock on the hillside.

Forgive, Choro . . .!

After the funeral feast, Samansur took Tanabai on one side.

"Tanake, I have something to tell you, we must have a talk."

They went across the yard, leaving the people, the smoking samovars and fires. They went out to the back into the garden. They walked along the edge of the irrigation ditch and stopped outside the village by an old fallen tree. They sat on it in silence with their thoughts.

"Such is life," thought Tanabai, "I knew Samansur as a little lad and now look what he has grown into. His grief has made him into a grown-up man. Now he has taken Choro's place and he and I are equals. That's how it should be. Sons take the place of their fathers. Sons carry on with the family, with the work. May God make him a man like his father. So that he may advance, and in wisdom and knowledge may rise higher than us, to create happiness for himself and for others. This is why we are fathers, this is why we beget sons, in the hope that they will be better than us; that's the whole purpose of life."

"You, Samansur, are the oldest in the family," began Tanabai, stroking his beard as old men do. "Now you have taken Choro's place and I am ready to listen to you as I listened to Choro."

"I must tell you, Tanake, about my father's command."

Tanabai shivered, hearing in the son's speech, the voice and intonation of the father and noticed for the first time that he was very like his father, the young Choro whom his son had never known, but whom Tanabai had known and remembered. Is not that why they say that a man does not die while there are men alive who knew him?

"I'm listening to you, my son."

"I got to my father's side while he was still alive. I arrived yesterday evening an hour before he died. He was conscious until his last breath. He was waiting for you to come, Tanake. All the time he was asking 'Where's Tanabai? Has he not come?' We consoled him, telling him that you were on your way, that you would soon appear. It was clear that he wanted to tell you about something. But he could not hang on."

"Yes, Samansur, yes. We should have seen one another again.

173

We should have done. I will never forgive myself. I am to blame. I did not arrive in time."

"This is what he told us to pass on to you. He said to me, 'My son, say to my Tanake that I ask for his forgiveness; tell him that he should not hold his resentment in his heart and that he himself should take my party card to the *raikom* and hand it in there with his own hand. Don't forget to tell him to do that.' Then he seemed to lose consciousness a bit, he was in pain. As he lay there, dying, it seemed as if he was waiting for someone. He just cried and we couldn't make out what he was saying."

Tanabai did not answer. He pulled at his beard, sobbing. Choro had gone. Choro had taken with him half of Tanabai himself, had taken away a part of his life.

"Thank you, Samansur, for telling me this. And thanks be to your father, too," he said at last, controlling himself as much as he could. "Only one thing troubles me. You know that they have expelled me from the party?"

"I know."

"Then how can I, no longer a member of the party, take Choro's card to the *raikom*? I've no right to do so."

"I don't know about that, Tanake. It is for you to decide. But I must fulfil the last wish of my father. I ask you to do as he wished, to do as he said when he left us."

"I would be glad in my soul to do so. But this disaster has come upon me. Would it not be better if you took it, Samansur?"

"No, it would not be better. My father knew what he was asking. If he trusted you, then why should I not trust in you. Tell them in the *raikom* that it was the wish of my father, Choro Sayakov."

It was still dark, early in the morning, when Tanabai rode out of the village. Gul'sary, the fine pacer Gul'sary, was in sorrow and in joy a sure-footed horse. Gul'sary struck with his hooves the frozen lumps of the earth track. This time he was carrying Tanabai, on the special task given to him by his dead friend, communist Choro Sayakov.

Ahead over the invisible edge of the earth, the light of dawn was coming up. In the middle of the light the new dawn was being born. It was growing there inside the grey mist . . .

The pacer was running towards the dawn, towards the single

174

bright star still shining there in the firmament. Alone on the desert road drummed the pacer's hooves. It was a long time since Tanabai had ridden him. Gul'sary's pace was as fast and even as ever. The wind flattened his mane and blew into his rider's face. Gul'sary was still in good fettle.

All the way Tanabai was wondering and guessing why Choro had ordered before his death that he alone—a man expelled from the party—should take his party card to the *raikom*. What did he want? Or was it a trial of strength for him? Perhaps in this way he wanted to express his disagreement with the expulsion of Tanabai from the party? Now no one will ever know the reason or ever be able to ask. Never again would he say anything. Yes, those are terrifying words, "Never again". There can be nothing after those words . . .

These various thoughts swept into his mind as they revived all that he had wished to expel from it for ever. No, it seemed as if all was not yet over. With him there was still Choro's last wish. He would come with the party card and explain about him, about Choro, about what had happened, what Choro meant to the people and to him. He would be telling the story of his own life, for he and Choro were like fingers from the same hand.

Let them know what they had been then, in their youth, what a life they had lived through. Perhaps then they would understand that Tanabai did not deserve to be divided by them from Choro, either in life or in death. If only they would hear him out, let him say all that he had to say.

Tanabai imagined how he would enter the office of the *raikom* secretary, how he would lay on the table Choro's party card and how he would tell everything. He would admit his guilt and apologise, if by that they would let him back into the party which he could not live without, and without which he could not imagine himself living.

Supposing they said, "What right have you, a man expelled from the party, to bring in a party document? You should not have touched the party card of a communist; you should not have taken on this task! There were others, not you, to do this!"

But had not this been the last wish of Choro himself, before he died! He had made this last wish in the presence of others, as he lay dying. His son, Samansur, could confirm this.

"Well, anyone could say such a thing as he lay dying, in his delirium." What would he answer then?

Gul'sary ran on over the ringing, frozen road, over the steppe and was already coming down the hill into Aleksandrovka. The pacer had carried Tanabai quickly and he had hardly noticed that they were already there.

The day's work was only just beginning in the offices as Tanabai arrived at the regional district centre. Without stopping elsewhere he took the sweating pacer directly to the *raikom* building, tied him up, brushed off the dust and went in with his heart pounding from excitement. What would they say to him? How would they receive him? There was no one in the corridors. No one had yet got in from the villages. Tanabai walked in to Kashkataev's outer office.

"Good morning!" he said to the secretary.

"Good morning!"

"Is comrade Kashkataev in?"

"Yes."

"I've come to see him. I'm a shepherd from the White Stones *kolkhoz*. My name is Bakasov," he began.

"Of course, we know of you," she smiled.

"Well then, please tell him that our *partorg*, Choro Sayakov, has died and his last request was that I should bring his party card to the *raikom*. And here I am."

"All right. Please wait a moment."

But although she was not long in Kashkataev's office, Tanabai had already gone through agonies, not knowing what to do as he waited for her return.

"Comrade Kashkataev is busy," she said firmly closing the door behind her. "He asked you to hand in Sayakov's party card at the registry. It is there, on the right and down the corridor."

"Registry, on the right down the corridor." What did this mean? Tanabai did not realise. Then he understood all at once and all at once his whole world collapsed. How could it be like that? Was it just so easy? And he had thought . . .

"But I have something to say to him. I beg you, please go and tell him that I have something important to say to him."

176

The secretary hesitated, but went into the office; coming back she again said, "He is very busy." Then she added sympathetically, "There is no more to be said," and then more quietly, "he won't see you. You had better go."

Tanabai went out into the corridor and turned to the right where he found the sign "Registry". There was a hatch in the door, so he knocked. The hatch opened.

"What do you want?"

"I have brought this party card to you. Our *partorg*, Choro Sayakov, has died. White Stones *kolkhoz*."

The woman in charge of the registry waited patiently while Tanabai got the leather case on its strap out of his coat; it was his own case in which, until recently, he had carried his own card and in this he had brought Choro's card. He handed over the card.

"Farewell, Choro!"

He watched as she wrote in the book the number of the party card, Choro's surname, first name and patronymic and the year he joined the party—a last memory of him. Then she gave him the book to sign.

"Is that all?" asked Tanabai.

"That's all."

"Good-bye."

"Good-bye."

The hatch slammed to.

Tanabai went out on to the street. He began to unhitch the pacer.

"That's all, Gul'sary," he said to the horse, "that's all."

The untiring pacer took him back to the village. The great wide steppe in spring glory raced towards him, to the sound of the breeze and the pacer's hooves. Only in the running of the horse did Tanabai's pain ease and quieten.

That same evening Tanabai came home to the mountains.

His wife met him in silence. She took hold of the horse's bridle. She helped her husband down with her arm under his.

Tanabai turned to her, took her in his arms and rested his head on her shoulder. She clung to him, crying.

"We have buried Choro. He is no more, Dzhaidar. My friend is no more," said Tanabai and once again gave way to his tears.

Then he went to sit on the stone by the *yurta*. He wanted to be alone, to watch the moon rise as it came up from behind the teeth-like peaks of the white, snow-covered range. In the *yurta* his wife was putting the children to bed. There was the sound of the fire crackling on the hearth. Then she began to sing a soul-catching tune as she played on the *temir-komuz*. It was as if the wind was howling, as if someone was running over the field crying and singing a sad song, while all around was quiet with the world holding its breath, there was only this silence; just the lonely voice running, this voice of melancholy and of a man's suffering. As if he was running and did not know where to hide with his grief, where to find comfort amongst the silence and loneliness with no one answering him. He was crying and only he was listening. Tanabai understood that his wife was playing for him "The Song of the Old Hunter"...

... Long ago an old man had a son—a young and cunning hunter. The father himself had taught him the difficult art of the hunt and his son had exceeded him in skill.

He did not know what it was to miss a shot. Not one living creature could escape his sure and death-bearing bullet. He killed all the game in the mountains around. He did not spare either the mothers bearing young or the young themselves. He destroyed the herd of the Grey She-goat, the mother of all goats. There remained the Grey She-goat with her old mate, the old Grey He-goat. She begged the young hunter to spare her old mate, the old He-goat, not to kill him, so that the race could continue. But the young hunter did not listen and killed the great Grey He-goat with a sure shot. The goat fell from the cliff. Then the Grey She-goat turned her side towards the hunter and said in her grief: "Shoot me in the heart. I will not move. But you will miss, and this will be the last shot of your life." The young hunter laughed at her, at the words of the mad old Grey She-goat. He took aim, a shot rang out. But the Grey She-goat did not fall. The bullet had struck her foreleg. The hunter was frightened, for nothing like this had happened to him before. "Now," said the Grey She-goat, "now try and catch me, lame as I am." Again the young hunter laughed at her in reply, "Then try to get away. I'll catch you and I'll show you no mercy. I will cut your throat, you boasting old creature."

178

The lame Grey She-goat began to run and the hunter after her. For many days and nights the chase went on, over cliffs, up slopes, over snow and rocks. The Grey She-goat did not give in. Long ago the hunter had thrown away his gun, all his clothes were in tatters. He had not noticed that the Grey She-goat had led him up to an inaccessible crag from which he could go neither up nor down, could not crawl away or jump to another ledge. Here the Grey She-goat left him and as she did she cursed him. "You will never escape from here and no one can save you. Let your father weep over you as I will weep over my dead young ones, over my vanished race. May your father howl here alone amongst these mountain rocks and I too will howl alone amongst the mountains. I the old Grey She-goat, the mother of all goats, I curse you, Karagul, I curse you." Weeping the Grey She-goat ran away leaping from rock to rock, from mountain to mountain.

The young hunter stayed there, left on the dizzy precipice, with his face to the rocky wall. He feared to look, he could go neither up nor down, to the left nor to the right. He could see neither the sky above nor the earth beneath.

Meanwhile his father was searching everywhere for him, all through the mountains. When he found the abandoned gun, he knew that some disaster had overtaken his son. He ran through the rocky gorges, among the dark clefts. "Karagul, where are you? Answer, Karagul!" And in answer the rocks of the mountains laughed a rocky laughter and answered him with his own words, "Where are you, Karagul? Answer!"

"Here I am, Father." Suddenly he heard a voice coming from somewhere high above. The father looked up and saw his son like a fledgling raven on the precipice edge, on a high inaccessible cliff. He stood there with his back to the world, unable to turn round.

"How did you get up there, my unhappy son?"

"Do not ask me, father. I am here as my punishment. The old Grey She-goat led me here and cursed me with a terrible curse. I have already been standing here many days and I can see neither sun nor sky nor earth. Never again will I see your face, father. Have pity on me, father. Kill me! End my suffering, I beg you. Kill and bury me."

What could the father do? He wept, he was in despair and all the while his son begged him: "Kill me quickly! Shoot, father! Pity me, shoot!" The father could not make up his mind. But before sunset he took aim and fired the shot. Then he broke his gun on a rock and sang the song of farewell over the body of his son.

> Now I have killed you, my son Karagul,
> I am alone on earth, my son Karagul.
> Fate has chastised me, my son Karagul.
> Fate has punished me, my son Karagul.
> Because I taught you, my son Karagul,
> The wise hunter's craft, my son Karagul.
> Because you killed all, my son Karagul,
> The fowl and creatures, my son Karagul.
> Because you destroyed, my son Karagul,
> All that lived and bred, my son Karagul.
> I am alone on earth, my son Karagul.
> No one will answer, my son Karagul,
> With their tears my tears, my son Karagul,
> Now I have killed you, my son Karagul,
> Killed with my own hands, my son Karagul . . .

. . . Tanabai sat there by the *yurta* and listened to the old Kirgiz mourning song and watched as the moon rose above the dark, silent mountains; and hung above the sharp, snow-covered peaks, above the vast, stony crags. Once more he begged his dead friend for forgiveness.

In the *yurta* Dzhaidar played on on the *temir-komuz* the mourning song about the great hunter, Karagul,

> Now I have killed you, my son Karagul,
> I am alone on earth, my son Karagul . . .

23

Dawn was approaching. As he sat by the fire at the head of the dying pacer, the old man, Tanabai, remembered what had happened next. No one knew that he had gone in those days to the *oblast'* town. It was his last endeavour. He wanted to see the *oblast'* committee secretary, whom he had heard speak at the meeting at region, and tell him about all his troubles. He was sure that this man would understand him and help him. Choro had spoken well of him and others had praised him too. It was only when he arrived there that he heard that the secretary had been transferred to another *oblast'*.

"Hadn't you heard?"

"No."

"Well, if your business is very important, I can tell our new secretary and perhaps he will see you," suggested the woman in the office.

"No thank you," said Tanabai, "I had wished to speak about private matters. The former secretary and I knew each other. But I will not worry the new man. Excuse me. Good-bye."

He left, believing in his heart that he had known the secretary and that the secretary knew him, the shepherd Bakasov, personally. Why not? They could have known and respected one another; he did not doubt this and had therefore spoken as he did.

Tanabai walked along the street towards the bus station. Near the beer kiosk, two workers were loading the empty beer barrels on to a lorry. One stood inside. The other lifting the barrels up to him looked around as Tanabai went past and froze on the spot and his expression changed. It was Bektai. Holding the barrel on the ramp, he looked at Tanabai for a long time with disgust in his narrow lynx-like eyes and waited for something to be said.

"What, have you gone to sleep?" the man in the truck called to Bektai.

The barrel slipped back a bit and as he caught it, Bektai bent under the weight and went on looking at Tanabai, but Tanabai gave him no greeting. "So here you are. Here you are. Well. No more to be said. Taken up the brewing business," thought Tanabai walking on without stopping. "Perhaps the boy could lose everything?" he thought and slowed down. "Or he could become a useful person. Perhaps I should have a word with him?" He wanted to go back; he had been sorry for Bektai, had been ready to forgive him if only the other would do the same. But he did not do that. He realised that if Bektai knew he had been expelled from the party, it would give this evil-tongued boy a chance to take it out on him, on his fate and on all that he was still faithful to. So he walked on.

He left the town by hitch-hiking a ride on a lorry and thought about Bektai. He remembered how he had stood there, taking the weight of the barrel and how he had looked at him in expectation.

Later when Bektai was on trial, Tanabai had only told the court that Bektai had abandoned his flock and left. He had not said any more. But he wished that Bektai would at last realise that he had done wrong and would acknowledge this. But it seemed Bektai did not wish to be sorry.

"When you've done your time, come and see me. We'll talk about what is to be done," Tanabai had said to Bektai. But the latter had not answered or even looked up. So Tanabai had left him. After he had been expelled from the party, he had lost his self-confidence and felt guilty before everyone. He was somehow scared. He had never thought that such a thing would happen to him. No one had ever thrown it in his teeth, but all the same he avoided people more and more, avoided talking and was more often silent.

24

The pacer Gul'sary lay motionless by the fire, his head on the ground. His life was slowly leaving him. There was a wheezing in his throat, his eyes were wide open and dimmed as they gazed without blinking at the flames; his legs were stiff and extended like sticks.

Tanabai said good-bye to his pacer, with these last words:

"You have been a great horse, Gul'sary. You have been my friend. You are taking away with you the best years of my life, Gul'sary. I shall always remember you, Gul'sary. Now I am remembering all about you because you are dying, my fine horse, my Gul'sary. One day we shall meet one another again in that other world, Gul'sary. But there I will not hear the music of your hooves. Because there there are no tracks, there is no earth, there is no grass, there is no life. But while I am alive you will not die, because I will remember you, Gul'sary. The sound of your hooves will always be my favourite music."

These were Tanabai's thoughts and he was sad because time was passing by like the running of the pacer. They had both grown old too quickly. Perhaps Tanabai thought of himself as an old man too soon. But a man grows old not so much because of his years, but from the realisation that he is growing old, that his time has passed, that he has only to live out the days left to him.

In this night while his pacer was dying, Tanabai again went over his whole past and was sorry that he had given in to age, that he had not decided to follow the advice of that man, who, so it turned out, had not forgotten about him but had searched him out and come to him again.

This had happened seven years after he had been expelled from the party. Tanabai was then on horse patrol duties, looking after the *kolkhoz* land in the Sarygousk ravine and living there in the watcher's hut with his old Dzhaidar. His daughters had left to study and then had got married. His son, after completing the course at the technical school, had started work in the regional town and was now also a family man.

Once Tanabai was mowing the grass on the stream bank in the summer. The day was a good one for haymaking, hot and bright. It was quiet in the ravine. The grasshoppers were trilling away. Tanabai was working with his shirt open, in his wide legged old man's trousers, following his ringing scythe, felling the grass in even, flat swathes. He was working with such pleasure that he had not noticed that a light Gaz van had stopped, that two people had got out of the vehicle and were coming across to him.

"Good morning, Tanake. May God help you." All at once he heard someone speaking beside him. He looked round and saw Ibraim. He was just the same, agile, fat-cheeked, with a slight paunch. "Well, we've found you," Ibraim was smiling all over his face, "the secretary of the *raikom* has come as he wanted to see you."

"Oh, the old fox!" Tanabai thought. "He always comes up on top. Look how he is fawning. He seems such a very kind person, helping anyone, working for anyone."

"Good morning." Tanabai shook hands with them.

"Don't you recognise me, father?" asked the comrade with Ibraim politely holding Tanabai's hand.

Tanabai did not hurry to answer—where had he seen him? In front of him stood a very familiar, but all the same a much changed man. Young, healthy, sunburnt, with an open, confident and honest way of looking at you; he was wearing a grey linen suit and a straw hat.

"Someone from the town," thought Tanabai.

"Of course you know him, it's comrade . . ." Ibraim wanted to prompt him.

"Wait, wait, I'll say it myself," Tanabai stopped him and then said, laughing at himself, "I recognise you, my son. How could I fail to recognise you! Good morning, again. I am glad to see you!"

It was Kerimbekov. That same *komsomol* secretary, who had so boldly taken Tanabai's part in the *raikom*, when they expelled him from the party.

'Well, as you've recognised me, let's have a talk, Tanake. We'll take a walk along the bank. In the meantime you can take the scythe and do a bit of work," Kerimbekov turned to Ibraim.

The latter readily agreed and took off his coat.

"With pleasure, of course, comrade Kerimbekov."

Tanabai and Kerimbekov walked over the meadow and sat down on some rocks by the stream.

"You have guessed, no doubt, Tanake, why I have come to see you," began Kerimbekov, "I see that you are still as strong as ever, you wield a scythe, that means there's nothing wrong with your health. I'm glad."

"I'm listening, my son, I'm glad about you, too."

"Well, let's make things plainer for you, Tanake. Now, as you yourself know, much has changed; already much has improved. You know this no less than I."

"I know. It's true. One can judge just here in our *kol-khoz*. Things have got so much better, that one can hardly believe it. Not long ago I was in the Valley of the Five Trees—where I suffered so much that year as a shepherd. I was envious. They've built a good lambing shed, a new one with a slate roof for fifteen hundred sheep. The shepherd has a house nearby and there are a barn and a stable. It's quite unlike it was in the old days and it's the same at the other wintering camps. In the village too, the people are busy building; wherever you go a new house has sprung up. God grant that this continues."

"That is what we are concerned about, Tanake. As yet not everything is as it should be, but in time we will get it right. Here's what I came to see you about. Return to the party! We will reconsider your case. There was a discussion at the bureau about you. As they say, better late than never."

Tanabai did not answer. He was confused. He was both glad and bitter. He remembered all the past, the resentment deep-rooted inside him. He did not wish to resurrect the past or think about it.

"Thank you for your kind words," said Tanabai to the *raikom* secretary. "Thank you for not forgetting an old man." Then after a moment's silence, he said, "I'm old. What use can the party get out of me now? What can I do for it? I'm no use. My time has passed. Don't be angry. Let me think it over."

Tanabai did not make any decision for a long time. He kept on putting things off: "Tomorrow I'll go, or the day after," and time went past. He was slow in getting going.

Once he had got everything ready, saddled his horse and rode off. But he came back after going half-way. But why? He realised that he was stupid to turn back. He had said to himself, "You're crazy, you've reached your second childhood." He realised all this but he could do nothing.

He had seen in the steppe the dust rising from a running horse's hooves. At once he had recognised Gul'sary. He hardly ever saw him now. The pacer was crossing the dry summer steppe leaving a white trail. As Tanabai watched from afar off he was sad. For formerly the dust from his hooves had never caught up with the pacer. He had raced on like a swift bird in flight, leaving behind him a long, swirling trail of dust. But now it was sometimes forming a cloud around the pacer. He would race ahead, but a minute later he disappeared again into the cloud of rising dust. No, he could no longer leave it far behind; he had got old and weak and had given up.

"Things are bad with you, Gul'sary," thought Tanabai with a twinge of sadness.

He imagined the horse choking from the dust, how hard it would be for him to run and how his angry rider would be whipping him. He could see the worried eyes of the horse and felt how he would be trying with all his strength to escape from the dust but would be unable to do so. Although the rider could not hear Tanabai, for he was a long way off, Tanabai shouted to him, "Stop, don't force your horse," and started to try and cut him off.

But he did not catch up, so he stopped quite soon. All would have been well, if the other had understood him, but if he had not, what then? Supposing he had said to him in answer, "What business is it of yours? Why do you set yourself up as a teacher of horsemanship? I'll ride how I like! Get lost, you old fool!"

Meanwhile the pacer had drawn further away with an uneven gait, sometimes disappearing into the dust cloud, then breaking away from it. Tanabai followed him with his gaze for a long while. Then he turned his horse round and rode back.

"We've both had our run, Gul'sary," he mused. "We've both

grown old and who needs us now? I cannot stand the pace either, all we have left now is to live out our span."

A year later Tanabai saw the pacer harnessed to a cart. This upset him again. It was sad to see such a fine riding horse going downhill and having to go around with a rotten, moth-eaten old collar around his neck and dragging a wretched cart. Tanabai turned away, he did not want to look.

Then on another occasion he saw the pacer again. A little boy of about seven, in trousers and a torn shirt, was riding him along the street, proud and delighted to be in charge of a horse, spurring him with his bare heels. It was clear that it was the first time he had ridden and so they had given him the quietest and most obedient old horse; so low had fallen the famous pacer, Gul'sary. "Grandad, look at me," boasted the little boy to the old man, "I'm Chapaev! I'll ride across the stream!"

"Go on! I'm watching you,' exclaimed Tanabai.

Boldly pulling at the reins, the boy went across the stream but when the horse began to climb up on to the other bank, he could not hold on and fell into the water.

"Ma-ma-a!" he yelled in fear. Tanabai pulled him out of the water and carried him to the horse. Gul'sary stood calmly on the path, shifting his weight on to one leg and then on to the other.

"His legs are shivering and chilled, that's bad," realised Tanabai. He put the boy back on to the old pacer.

"Off you go and don't fall off again!"

Gul'sary wandered off quietly along the path.

Now even though the pacer had again come back into Tanabai's hands and it had appeared that the old man had got him back on to his feet, it seemed that Gul'sary had taken him for the very last time to Aleksandrovka and was now dying by the roadside.

Tanabai had gone to see his son and daughter-in-law after the birth of a grandson, their second child. He had taken with him a lamb, a sack of potatoes, bread and various bits of food cooked by his wife.

He understood later on why Dzhaidar had not wanted to go and had said that she felt ill. Although she never said as much, she did not like her daughter-in-law. In any case their son was not very independent, with no will of his own, and had got for himself a harsh, strong-willed wife. She sat at home, gave orders and bossed her husband as she wished. There are such people in the world who can easily insult, give offence to a person, just to feel that they have the upper hand and exercise their power.

It happened just like that on this occasion. It turned out that their son had been expecting promotion at his work, but then someone else was put up for it and he was passed over. So she waded in against the innocent old man.

"Why did you have to join the party, if all you were going to do was to spend your life as a shepherd or a herdsman? In the end they threw you out all the same and now your son cannot get anywhere in his work. So he'll sit in the same place for a hundred years, in the same post. You live up there in the mountains—what more do you old people want? We just have to suffer down here because of you."

Etcetera, etcetera, etcetera, all in that vein.

Tanabai was sorry that he had come. In order to calm down his daughter-in-law, he said mildly and uncertainly:

"There is a possibility that I will ask to rejoin the party."

"What do you want to go and do that for? Are they waiting for you to do so? Can't they get on without an old man like you?" she giggled in answer.

If it had not been his daughter-in-law, the wife of his own son, but someone else Tanabai would not have allowed them to get away with talking to him like that. But there's nothing that you can do about your own family, be they good or bad. The old man said nothing. He did not contradict her, did not say that her husband had not been promoted—not because of his father—but because he was useless and he had got himself a wife from whom even a saint would have run miles away. As they say, "A good wife will make a bad husband into an average one, an average one into a good one, and will make a good one world renowned."

But he did not wish to shame his son in front of his wife; let them think that he was to blame.

So Tanabai had left as quickly as he could. It made him sick even to be with them.

188

"You foolish girl, you foolish girl," he said swearing at his daughter-in-law, as he sat by the fire. "Who created such a one as you? You wish neither honour, respect or good to anyone else. All that you do is to look after yourself. You judge everyone by your own standards. Only things won't be as you wish. I am still needed; I will still be needed . . ."

Morning came. The mountains towered over the earth and as it got lighter more and more of the steppe was to be seen. On the edge of the ravine, the brown ashes of the dying fire were just smouldering. Beside it stood the old, grey-haired man with the coat flung over his shoulders. Now there was no longer any need to cover his horse. Gul'sary had gone to another world, to God's own herds ...

Tanabai looked at the fallen horse and was still stunned by what had happened to him. Gul'sary lay on his side with his head thrown back in death. It bore the deep scars of the bridle. His fine straight legs were stretched out, showing the worn shoes on the cracked hooves. No more would they ring out on the earth, no more leave their mark on the road. Tanabai had to go on. He bent over his horse for the last time, closed the cold lids over the eyes, picked up the bridle, and without turning for another look, went away.

He walked across the steppe towards the mountains. As he walked he was alone with his thoughts. He thought how old he now was, how his days were drawing to their end. He did not want to die like a lone bird which had strayed away from his fellows in a fast flying skein. He wanted to die in full flight so that those with whom he had grown up in the same nest, with whom he had travelled the same way, should be around him to call him farewell.

"I will write to Samansur," decided Tanabai, "I will write this—Do you remember the pacer, Gul'sary? You certainly should do. It was on his back that I rode to take your father's party card to the *raikom*. You yourself asked me to go on that errand. Well, last night on the way home from Aleksandrovka my wonderful pacer lay down and died. I sat there the whole night beside him and lived my whole life over again. The time is not far off when I, too, must die by the road, like Gul'sary. You must help me, Samansur, my son, to come back to the party. I've only a little time left. I want to be back again with those with whom I have always been. As I now understand, your father Choro had good reasons to wish that I should take his card to the *raikom*. You are his son, you know me, the old man Tanabai Bakasov."

Tanabai walked on over the steppe with the bridle slung over his shoulder. Tears flooded down his cheeks and wetted his beard. But he did not wipe them away. They were his tears for the pacer Gul'sary. The old man looked through his tears at the new day, at a lone grey goose flying fast and high over the foot-hills. The goose was racing after it's skein.

"Fly on, fly on," whispered Tanabai. "Catch up with your flock, before your wings tire . . ." Later on he sighed and said:

"Farewell, Gul'sary!"

*   *   *

He walked on and he remembered the old song:
   "The camel runs for many days.
   She seeks and calls for her young one.
   Where are you, little black-eyed camel? Answer me!
   The milk is flowing from my teats, from the full udder
      and down the legs.
   Where are you? Answer me.
   The milk is flowing from my teats, from the full udder . . .
      White milk . . ."